Burning Terror

In Part 1, John Saul introduced us to the village of Blackstone, where a dark figure prowled the hidden rooms of the old Asylum and found the talismans of evil with which to enact an unspeakable terror. First came the antique doll, which tore apart the young family of the local contractor, Bill McGuire.

In Part 2, the president of the First National Bank of Blackstone, Jules Hartwick, found a beautifully wrapped package in his wife's car. The silver locket inside unleashed a murderous, maniacal rage.

Now, deep inside the Asylum, a gloved hand selects a cigarette lighter in the shape of a dragon. It will ignite a fiery and very deadly reunion. . . .

THE BLACKSTONE CHRONICLES
ASHES TO ASHES:
THE DRAGON'S FLAME

THE BLACKSTONE CHRONICLES

PART 3
ASHES TO ASHES: THE DRAGON'S FLAME

John Saul

FAWCETT CREST • NEW YORK

A Fawcett Crest Book
Published by Ballantine Books
Copyright © 1997 by John Saul

Map by Christine Levis

All rights reserved under International and Pan-American Copyright Conventions. Published in the United States by Ballantine Books, a division of Random House, Inc., New York, and simultaneously in Canada by Random House of Canada Limited, Toronto.

http://www.randomhouse.com

Library of Congress Catalog Card Number: 96-90777

ISBN 0-449-22786-3

Manufactured in the United States of America

First Edition: April 1997

10 9 8 7 6 5 4 3 2 1

For Linda with
peaches and cream

✳

Prelude

*I*t was the kind of wintry March night that kept all but the most restless of Blackstone's citizens nestled within the warmth of their homes. Though the temperature hovered just above freezing, the wind that crept up on the town just after nightfall brought with it a chill of its own. Its gusts gathered force throughout the night, unleashing a howling monster that tore branches from the bare trees, clawed shingles from the roofs, and rattled at the windows of every house, as if searching for ways to enact its fury upon the people within. Clouds, torn to shreds by the raging wind, scudded across the sky in grayish tatters, swirling across the moon so that dark shadows moved through the streets like thieves slithering from house to house.

In the Asylum atop North Hill the dark figure was oblivious to the menace of the night. Inured to the moaning of the wind and not feeling the cold, he crouched in his chamber, lovingly fingering the golden dragon. Its ruby red eyes seemed to blink with every darkening of the moon beyond the room's single tiny window. Cradling the dragon in his gloved hands, he cast his mind back to the time when he had first laid eyes on it. . . .

✳

Prologue

It wasn't right.

It wasn't the way it was supposed to have been.

When she'd discovered she was pregnant, Tommy was supposed to insist that they get married immediately.

But instead of putting his arms around her and assuring her that everything would be all right, he'd looked at her with such pure fury blazing in his eyes that she thought he was going to hit her, that he would throw her out of the roadster right then, and she'd have to walk all the way home. "How could you be so stupid?" he demanded. They were parked on the lovers' lane on the slope of North Hill that faced away from Blackstone, and he'd yelled so loud that the people in the backseat of the only other car up there that night had rubbed a clear spot in the steamy window and peered curiously over at them.

She'd shrunk down in the seat, so embarrassed she wanted to die. Then Tommy started the engine and took off, slamming the car through the curves so fast she was terrified they were both going to get killed before they got back to town.

Maybe that would have been better than what happened next. He pulled up in front of her house, reached across and shoved the door open, then glowered at her one last time. "Don't think I'm going to marry you," he growled. "In fact, don't even think you're going to see me again!"

Sobbing, she stumbled out of the car, and he roared

away, tires squealing, and disappeared around the corner. A week later, when she heard that Tommy had joined the army and was going to Korea, she knew she had no choice. She had to tell her parents.

She expected her dad to go into a rage, threatening to kill whoever did this to his little girl. When she told him Tommy was in the army, his face blackened with fury and he swore that if the North Koreans didn't kill the stinking son-of-a-bitch coward, he would, no matter how long it took. Her mother demanded to know how a daughter of hers could ever let a man use her the way Tommy had, and sobbed that she would never again be able to look any of her friends in the face.

All of that, she had expected.

What she hadn't expected was what happened the next day: Her parents took her up to the top of North Hill and committed her to the Asylum.

She sobbed and begged. She raged at her father with every bit as much fury as he'd raged at her the day before.

But her parents were implacable. She would stay in the Asylum until the baby was born.

Only then would they decide what would be best for her to do next.

For the first two months, she lived in terror, afraid even to leave her room for fear of what might happen to her. All her life she and her friends had lived in quiet fear of the building at the top of North Hill. All through her childhood there were whispered stories of terrible things that went on up there, and she'd spent more than one sleepless night cowering under her quilt at rumors that one of the "lunatics" had escaped.

The first few nights in the Asylum were the worst. She was unable to sleep, for here there was no quiet at night; instead the hours of darkness were alive with the screams and moans of the tormented souls hidden away within the forbidding stone walls. But slowly her mind became inured to the howls of anguish that echoed through the small hours of the night. Finally she began to venture forth into the dayroom, where she joined the rest of the lower security patients, who whiled away their lives playing endless games of solitaire or thumbing through magazines whose pages they never actually read.

And they smoked.

During her second month in the dayroom, she began smoking too. It passed the time, and somehow numbed the pain of loneliness and hopeless desperation.

As the weeks turned into months, and her belly swelled with the child she was carrying, she began slowly, tentatively to make friends with some of the patients. She even tried to befriend the woman who always sat perfectly still, only her constantly darting eyes betraying her consciousness. But the woman never spoke to her.

One day, the silent woman simply vanished, and though there were stories that the woman had died somewhere in the secret chambers rumored to be hidden deep in the Asylum's basement, she didn't quite believe the talk.

Nor did she quite disbelieve it.

Her family had not come to see her. That was no surprise: Her father was far too angry, her mother too ashamed.

And her two little sisters, both much younger than she, would be far too frightened to brave a visit to the Asylum on their own.

So the months passed.

Today, on a cold March morning after a night in which the howling of the wind had been loud enough to drown out the cries and wails of the Asylum's occupants, she felt the first painful contraction.

She winced as it gripped her body, but didn't let herself cry out, for over the months of her pregnancy she had come to understand that the pain of childbirth would be nothing more than punishment for the sin she and Tommy had committed.

A punishment she had vowed to bear in silence.

Within an hour, though, the contractions were coming every few minutes, and she could no longer bear the pain without crying out. The women in the dayroom called out to one of the orderlies, and the orderly summoned a nurse.

With the pains coming every two minutes, and her body feeling as if it was about to be torn apart, she was strapped onto a gurney and wheeled into a white-tiled room. From the ceiling, three brilliant lights blazed down, nearly blinding her.

The room was cold—close to freezing. The orderlies began to strip her gown from her body. She begged them not to.

They ignored her.

The nurse came in, and the doctor.

As yet another contraction racked her body, she begged them to give her something for the pain, but they only went about their work, ignoring her pleas. "It's not an operation," the doctor curtly told her. "You don't need anything."

Her labor intensified, and then she was screaming, and thrashing against the restraints that held her strapped to the gurney. It seemed to go on forever, wave after wave of pain so intense she was certain she would pass out, until, with one last agonizing spasm, she felt the baby slip from her body.

She lay gasping, trying to catch her breath, her exhausted body still at last. Then she heard it: a tiny, helpless cry. Her baby, the baby for whom she had endured unimaginable pain, was crying out to her.

"Let me see it," she whispered. "Let me hold my baby."

The doctor, his back to her, handed something to the nurse. "It's better you don't," he said. "Better for both of you."

The nurse left the room, and she heard her baby's wails fade away into the distance.

"No!" she cried out, but her voice was pitifully weak. "I have to see my baby! I have to hold it!"

The doctor finally looked at her. "I'm afraid I can't let you do that. It would only make it much harder for you."

She blinked. Harder? What was he talking about? "I—I don't understand—"

"If you don't see it, you won't miss it nearly as much."

"Miss it?" she echoed. "What are you talking about? Please! My baby—"

"But it's not your baby," the doctor said as if talking to a small child. "It's being given up for adoption, so it's better that you not see it at all."

"Adoption?" she echoed. "But I don't want to give—"

"What you want doesn't matter," the doctor informed her. "The decision has been made."

Now a new kind of pain flooded over her—not the sharp pangs of the contractions, which, as violently as they'd seized her body, had quickly dissipated. This was a dull ache that she felt taking root deep within her, which she knew was never going to fade—a spreading coldness that would grow inside her cancerously, filling her with despair, slowly consuming her, leaving her no avenue of escape. She could already feel it uncoiling inside her, and someday, she knew, there would be nothing left of her at all.

There would be nothing left but the pain of knowing that somewhere there was a baby who belonged to her, whom she would never nurse, never hold, never see.

Left alone in the operating room under the cold, merciless lights, she began to cry.

No one came to comfort her.

When she awakened the next morning, she was back in her room, and though her blanket was wrapped close around her, it did nothing to protect her from the icy chill that had spread through her body.

Though she felt utterly exhausted, something drew her from her bed to the window. The landscape beyond the bars was no less bleak than the Asylum's interior: naked gray branches clawed at a leaden sky. Only a wisp of smoke that curled from the chimney of the incinerator behind the Asylum's main building disturbed the cold, silent morning. She was about to turn away when a movement caught her eye—a nurse and an orderly emerging from the Asylum and walking toward the incinerator. It was the same nurse who had been in the operating room yesterday, and the orderly was one of the two who had strapped her to the gurney.

The nurse was carrying an object wrapped in what looked like a small blanket, and even though she could see nothing of what was hidden within the blanket's folds, she knew what it was.

Her baby.

They weren't putting it up for adoption at all.

She wanted to turn away from the window, but something held her there, some need to see exactly what was going to happen, even though the scene had already played itself out in her mind. In the next few moments, as she stood shivering with cold and desperate fear, the scene she had just imagined unfolded before her eyes:

The orderly opened the access port of the incinerator, and the flames within the combustion chamber suddenly flared, tongues of fire licking hungrily at the iron lips of the door. As she watched, the nurse unfolded the blanket.

She beheld the pale, still form of the child she'd brought into the world only the day before.

A scream of anguish built in her throat, erupting in an agonized wail as the orderly closed the incinerator door, mercifully blocking her view of what had been done to her baby. As they turned away from the incinerator, both the nurse and the orderly glanced up at her window, but if they recognized her, neither of them gave any sign. A moment later they too vanished from view.

For a long time she remained at the window, gazing out at the lonely, lifeless landscape that now seemed a perfect reflection of the coldness and emptiness inside her.

Her own fault.

All her own fault.

She should never have told her parents about the baby, never have let them bring her here, never have let them make the decisions that should have been hers.

And now, because of what she'd done, her baby was dead.

At last she turned away from the window, and now her body, as well as her spirit, felt numb. As if in a dream, she left her room and went to the dayroom. Seating herself in one of the hard, plastic-covered chairs, she stared straight ahead, looking at no one, speaking to no one. Hours passed. Sometime late in the afternoon a nurse came into the dayroom and placed a small package in her lap.

"Someone left this for you. A little girl."

It wasn't until long after the nurse had gone that she finally opened the package. She peeled the paper away. Inside was a small box. She opened the box and gazed at the object inside.

It was a cigarette lighter.

Made of a gold-colored metal, it was worked into the shape of a dragon's head, and when she pressed a trigger hidden in its neck, a tongue of flame shot out of the dragon's mouth.

Click. There were the flames that had shot hungrily from the mouth of the incinerator. Click. The fire leaped and consumed her baby.

She held the flame to her arm, and though her nostrils quickly filled with the sickly smell of burning flesh, she felt nothing.

No heat.

No pain.

Nothing at all.

Slowly, methodically, she began moving the dragon's flame over her skin, letting the fiery tongue lick at every exposed piece of her flesh, as if its heat could burn away the guilt that was consuming her.

As the rest of the patients in the dayroom silently watched, she burned herself—arms, legs, neck, face— until at last there was no more flesh to torture.

The dragon, its flame finally extinguished, was still clutched in her hand when the orderlies finally came and took her away.

Within the hour, her own body had joined her baby's.

The dark figure's gloved hand closed on the dragon, and he smiled.

It was time.

Time for the dragon, after nearly half a century hidden in this dark lair, to emerge once more into the world beyond these cold stone walls.

Chapter 1

Oliver Metcalf turned up his collar, huddled deeper into his old car coat, and glanced up at the sky, which was rapidly filling with rain clouds. It was Sunday, and he'd intended to spend the afternoon in the *Chronicle* office, catching up on the unending details that always managed to pile up until they threatened to overwhelm the newspaper's small staff, no matter how hard they worked. He was wading through a sea of paperwork when, an hour ago, Rebecca Morrison had turned up with a shy smile and the suggestion that he give up his boring old work in favor of accompanying her out to the flea market that had taken over the old drive-in theater on the western edge of town. Her eagerness was infectious, and Oliver quickly decided that none of the bills and correspondence that had waited for his attention this long couldn't wait a day or two longer. Now, however, as he shivered in the chill of the late March day, he wondered if he hadn't made a mistake. They were still two blocks from the drive-in, and it seemed the sky might open up with a downpour at any moment. "How come they're open so early? Aren't they afraid they'll get rained out?"

Rebecca smiled serenely. "They won't," she said. "It's the very first day, and it never rains on the first day of the flea market."

"That's the Rose Parade," Oliver corrected her. "And that's on New Year's Day, in California, where it never rains. Unless it's flooding, of course."

"Well, it's not going to rain today," Rebecca assured him. "And I like the flea market on the first day. It's when all the things people find in the attic or the basement over the winter are for sale."

Oliver shrugged. As far as he was concerned, one man's junk wasn't another man's treasure at all: it just became someone else's junk for a while. There was one item he'd been eyeing for years now—a truly ugly porcelain table lamp, embellished with strange vines that snaked up from its gilt-painted base and were studded with pieces of purple, red, and green colored glass meant to look like grapes. The lamp was topped by a hideous stained-glass shade—three pieces cracked, at last count— intended to suggest the spreading leaves of the vine. When lit, the light filtering through the leaf-form glass cast a shade of sickly green that made anyone within its glow look deathly ill. So far, Oliver had seen it on three different tables at the flea market, watched as it was sold no fewer than four times at the Blackstone Historical Society Auction, and even found it displayed for a couple of days in the window of an antique shop—not, blessedly, Janice Anderson's. "Just promise me you won't buy the grape lamp," he asked.

"Oh, I already did." Rebecca giggled. "I bought it two years ago. I was going to give it to someone as a joke, but the more I looked at it, the less funny it seemed. So I gave it to the Historical Society."

"Did anyone buy it at the auction?" Oliver asked.

"You bet!" Rebecca said. "Madeline Hartwick snapped it right up! Of course, she only bought it because she knew I'd donated it and was afraid I'd be hurt if nobody bid on it." Her eyes clouded. "Do you think she's going to be all right?" Rebecca asked, her voice anxious.

"It's going to take a while," Oliver replied. Madeline was finally out of the hospital now, but still hadn't recovered from the terrifying night when her husband, Jules, almost killed her, and succeeded in killing himself. She and her daughter, Celeste, were staying in Boston with Madeline's sister. Oliver wondered if Madeline would ever come back to the big house at the top of Harvard Street.

The strangest thing was that no one yet knew exactly why Jules Hartwick had killed himself, nor had Oliver been able to fathom exactly what the banker had meant when he'd uttered his last words:

"You have to stop it . . . before it kills us all."

Stop what? Jules had said nothing else before he'd died on the steps of the Asylum. Though Oliver had asked Madeline and Celeste what Jules could possibly have meant, neither woman had any idea. Oliver inquired of others as well—Andrew Sterling, who had been at the house that terrible night; Melissa Holloway at the bank; Jules's attorney, Ed Becker. But no one had come up with an answer.

Only Oliver's uncle, Harvey Connally, had even ventured a guess. "Do you suppose he thought there was some connection between what happened to him and poor Elizabeth McGuire's suicide?" his uncle mused. "But that doesn't make much sense, does it? After all, even though Jules and Bill McGuire are some kind of shirttail cousins, Jules wasn't related to Elizabeth at all. From what I remember of *her* family, pretty much all of them were crazy, one way or another. But that didn't have anything to do with Jules. His parents were steady as a rock, both of them." The old man had sighed. "Well, I don't suppose we'll ever know, will we?"

So far, Harvey Connally had been proved right; no one yet had the slightest idea what had provoked Jules Hartwick's sudden mental breakdown and suicide. Even the problems at the bank were getting straightened out, and though they weren't all settled yet, nobody was saying that Jules had done anything illegal. Imprudent, perhaps, but the bank was in no danger of failing, and he'd been in no danger of being disciplined, either by the bank's board or by the Federal Reserve auditors.

"I keep feeling like I should have done something," Rebecca said, unconsciously slipping her hand into Oliver's as they neared the outskirts of Blackstone and the sagging stockade fence that had once protected the patrons of the drive-in movie from the glaring headlights of cars passing in and out of town on Main Street. "Maybe instead of praying with Aunt Martha, I should have—" She faltered for a moment, then looked helplessly up at Oliver. "Doesn't it seem like I should have done *some*thing?"

"I don't think there was anything anyone could do," Oliver told her, giving her hand a reassuring squeeze. "And I don't think we'll ever know exactly what happened that night." He put on a bright smile and changed the subject. "So, are we looking for something special, or are we just browsing to see what people are throwing out this year?"

"I want to find a present for my cousin," Rebecca told him.

"Andrea?" Oliver asked. "Do you even know where she is?"

"She's coming home."

"Home?" Oliver echoed. "You mean to your aunt's house?"

Rebecca nodded. "She called Aunt Martha the day before yesterday, and said she didn't have anywhere else to go."

Oliver remembered the last time he'd seen Andrea Ward. It was twelve years ago, the day before her eighteenth birthday, and Andrea had been talking about nothing except getting away from her mother.

Her mother, and Blackstone too.

Oliver had been sitting at the soda fountain in the drugstore near the square when Andrea and a couple of her friends had come in. Barely even noticing he was there, they'd huddled together on the three stools at the soda fountain's corner, and he was treated to at least one teenager's view of Blackstone.

"I can't believe I've survived this long," Andrea had said, impatiently brushing her long mane of blond hair away from her face, only to groan in exasperation a moment later as it fell right back over her forehead. "And the first thing I'm going to do is get this cut off. Can you believe my mother actually thinks it's a sin to cut your hair?" Then, with a brittle laugh, she proceeded to recite the long list of things Martha Ward had proclaimed sinful. "There's dancing and drinking and going to movies, just for starters. And smoking, of course," she added, lighting a cigarette with a defiant flourish. "And let's not forget dating either. How am I supposed to find a husband if I can't have a date?"

"Maybe she wants you to go to college," one of her friends suggested, but Andrea only laughed again.

"All she wants me to do is pray, just like she does," the girl declared. As she brushed her hair off her face again, Oliver had glimpsed how pretty she was, despite the heavy makeup she wore.

Or she would have been pretty, if she wasn't so angry. But Andrea had been angry for a long time, and over the years her anger had manifested itself in clothes that showed off her figure a little too perfectly, and makeup that hardened her face rather than accentuated its beauty.

And though she was forbidden to date, she'd always been popular with Blackstone's teenage boys.

Far too popular, according to Martha Ward.

Having heard Andrea's diatribe, when she disappeared from Blackstone the next day, leaving nothing behind except a note saying she'd gone to Boston and was never coming back, Oliver hadn't been surprised.

Martha Ward had been.

She'd been both surprised and furious. On the single occasion nearly three years ago, when Andrea had finally returned to visit Blackstone with her live-in boyfriend in tow, Martha refused to see her.

"I do not countenance sin," she proclaimed. "Don't come back until you've either married him or left him."

Andrea had not been seen in Blackstone since.

"What happened?" Oliver asked now, as he and Rebecca turned onto the grounds of the old drive-in movie and surveyed the two dozen tables that had been set up—only a third of what there would be later in the spring and in the summer, when the weather had warmed and the tourists began coming through.

"Her boyfriend left her, and she lost her job," Rebecca said. "I guess she really doesn't have anyplace else to go. So I thought I'd try to find something to cheer her up."

They meandered among the tables for a while, stopping now and then to wonder at some of the items that some people seemed to think other people might want. One of the tables was covered with tiny people constructed out of pebbles that had been glued together and painted with happy faces. PEBBLE PEOPLE, a small, badly lettered card on the table proclaimed. TO KNOW THEM IS TO LOVE THEM. To know them is to loathe them, Oliver thought, but kept silent, guessing that the elderly woman sitting hopefully behind the table had made the weird little humanoids herself.

Another table contained a collection of light-switch plates to which dozens of rhinestones had been glued, and yet another displayed religious icons constructed out of tiny shells.

None of it, they decided, was right for Andrea.

And then, sitting on a table that Janice Anderson was tending, they found it. Rebecca spotted it first, half hidden behind an antique picture frame that had a chip on it, thus disqualifying it from being displayed in Janice's shop on Main Street. "Look!" Rebecca cried. "Isn't it wonderful?"

Oliver looked curiously at the object in Rebecca's

hand. At first he wasn't quite sure what it was. It seemed to be a dragon's head, which Rebecca was holding by the neck. Two red eyes glared out from deep sockets. When Rebecca squeezed the dragon's neck, Oliver saw a spark deep in its throat, immediately followed by a flame that shot out of its mouth.

"It's a cigarette lighter," Rebecca exclaimed. "Isn't it perfect?"

"How do you know Andrea still smokes?" Oliver asked.

"Because I heard Aunt Martha telling her she couldn't smoke anywhere in the house." Rebecca's expression clouded. "That's why I want to give her this. She already feels terrible about the way her life is going, and now Aunt Martha wants her to feel bad about smoking too. At least I can let her know that *I* don't disapprove of everything she does." The flame died away as Rebecca eased her grip on the lighter. She held the lighter out to Oliver, and he reached out to take it from her, but the instant his fingers touched the metal of its snout, he reflexively jerked them away as if they'd been burned.

"Be careful!" Rebecca cautioned. With one fingertip she touched the dragon's snout herself. It was barely warm. "He must have bitten you, Oliver," she said. "It's not hot at all." Smiling, she dropped the cigarette lighter into Oliver's hand.

Just as Rebecca had told him, the lighter now felt perfectly cool. But that was impossible: it had been burning hot just a second before. As he turned the strange object over, searching for its price, he wondered whether the odd sensation of heat he'd just felt was a sign—like the troubling headaches he'd been having—of something wrong. Very wrong. Lost in his disturbing thoughts, he barely noticed that Janice Anderson had finished with the customer she'd been waiting on and turned to them. At a nudge from Rebecca, Oliver recovered himself and held out the lighter. "How much for the dragon?" he asked.

Janice gazed blankly at the object Oliver was holding. "Are you sure this was on my table?" she said.

Oliver nodded. "Right there, next to that frame."

Frowning, Janice took the cigarette lighter and examined it from every angle. There was a trade name stamped on the bottom, but it was far too worn to be legible. Though at first glance it appeared to be gold, she could see that the cheap plating was starting to peel away; and the "ruby" eyes were obviously glass, maybe even plastic. The question was, Where had it come from? She had no memory of having bought it, nor even of picking it up from the back-room clutter now spread out on the table in front of her. But then, surveying some of the other junk on the table, she realized she didn't know where most of these bits and pieces had come from. Many were the odds and ends purchased in lots from estate sales. Others, she could have bought from any one of the dozens of people who had come into her shop over the last year, offering for sale treasure they'd found hidden in their attics. Usually, Janice simply turned them away, but now and then, when she sensed that someone was selling something out of desperate need, she would knowingly buy a worthless object, simply as a way of allowing its bearer to keep his dignity and pocket a dollar or two.

That, undoubtedly, was how the lighter had come into her possession, she now decided, even though she had no memory of it. But how much might she have paid for it? Five dollars? Perhaps ten? "Twenty?" she suggested, knowing there was no chance Oliver would agree to her first price. To her dismay, it was Rebecca Morrison who replied without a second's hesitation.

"I'll take it! It's just the kind of thing Andrea will love!"

"For twenty dollars?" Janice Anderson heard herself say. "You will *not* take it for twenty dollars, Rebecca. It certainly isn't worth more than ten, and if you ask me, seven-fifty would be closer to fair."

"Great!" Oliver said. "How about five? Or would you like to counter at two-fifty?"

Janice tried to glare at him, but found herself laughing instead. "How about we stick to the seven-fifty my honest side thinks it's worth?"

Before she could change her mind, Oliver paid for the dragon's head lighter, and Janice wrapped it up for Rebecca in a piece of tissue paper.

"You really think your cousin will like it?" Oliver asked as they left the flea market a few minutes later.

"Of course she will," Rebecca assured him. Her face was alight with pleasure at her find. "It really is just perfect for her."

Oliver hoped that if Andrea shared his and Janice's judgment about the aesthetics of the lighter, the young woman would be kind enough to keep her thoughts to herself.

$*$

Chapter 2

Andrea Ward moved nervously through the house she had grown up in and wondered how so many years could have passed with so little evidence of change.

The same drab furniture stood in the living room with antimacassars to protect the arms and backs of the horsehair upholstery still in place, though Andrea estimated that there hadn't been a guest in the house in at least twenty years.

Heavy curtains, the same ones that had hung at the windows when she was a child, still cut out all but the faintest rays of daylight, plunging the room into a deep gloom that obscured the fact that the wallpaper was faded and buckling, and the paint on the ceiling was peeling badly. It was dingier even than she remembered, in an even shabbier state of neglect, but otherwise exactly as depressing—and that was no surprise. Her mother never changed and nothing in her mother's house ever changed. All was exactly as it had been on the day she left. Even the chapel, with its dense, incense-laden air and garish statuary. Once, Andrea recalled, it had been her father's den, a cozy room with a thick shag rug, redolent with the inviting aroma of her father's cherry-flavored pipe tobacco.

But no more. Though she had been only five, Andrea could still remember as clearly as if it had been yesterday the morning Mr. Corelli, who ran the junk store, had arrived with his truck. At first she'd thought he must be looking for his daughter, Angela, who was her best friend back then. But she was wrong. Instead, Mr. Corelli carried all the furniture out of her father's den and loaded it into his truck. Andrea had pleaded with her mother, begged her to make Mr. Corelli put the furniture back: her daddy would be angry when he came home and found his den empty. That was when her mother told her that her father wasn't ever coming back.

"Even if he wants to, I won't have him," Martha had finished. "Your father is a tool of Satan, and I won't have him in my house again!"

Within a week, Fred Ward's snug sanctuary had been transformed into a retreat of another sort—her mother's chapel, where the little girl prayed just as hard as Martha did, begging God and the saints for her father to come home. For a long time she daydreamed while pretending to be rapt in prayer—pastel fantasies of her father taking her away from her mother's house, this cold, dark place that seemed to get darker and colder with every passing year. He would take her to live with him, in Paris, maybe, or in an orange grove in California, or on a sunny Caribbean beach.

But Fred Ward never did come back.

After Andrea ran away from Blackstone, she made an attempt to find him, searching the telephone directories in Boston and Manchester and even as far away as New York. But her resources were limited, and he seemed to have completely disappeared. Over the years, she had drifted from place to place, from one unsatisfying job to another, and into a succession of dead-end romances. Somehow, something always went wrong. Until, three years ago, she had met Gary Fletcher, who gave her a job as a waitress in the restaurant he managed. He was ten years older than she was. Handsome. Sexy. And in love with her.

Or so he said.

Until a month ago, when she'd told him she was pregnant. She'd been sure that they'd finally get married, and move out of their apartment and into a house, and for the first time she'd have a real family.

That was when he told her he couldn't marry her because of the simple fact that he'd never divorced his wife.

Andrea hadn't even known he'd been married.

The next day, instead of filing for a divorce from his wife, he kicked her out of their apartment.

The day after that, he fired her from the only job she'd ever managed to hang onto.

And the day after that, he withdrew all her savings from their joint checking account.

Panicked, Andrea tried to get another job, but was turned down at every interview she pursued. She tried to find a place to live, but she had no money. There were no friends to turn to: Gary had been her whole life.

With nowhere to turn, there was nothing to do but to swallow what little pride she had left and go home to Blackstone to try to start her life all over again.

First she would find a job—any job.

Then she would go back to school—and this time not quit until she'd finished.

And the next man she got involved with was going to have to be a lot more honest than Gary Fletcher had been.

Not rich.

Not even handsome.

Just honest, and decent, and willing to be a father to their kids. With these, the first hopeful thoughts she'd had in weeks, lightening her despair, Andrea had pulled her battered Toyota into the familiar driveway on Harvard Street, and breathed a sigh of relief when she realized that no one was home. She would not have to face her mother—yet.

The old key she had never quite had the courage to toss out still fit the lock. Inside, it was oppressive and dark—even darker and more oppressive than she remembered it. Now, wandering through the downstairs rooms, noting their unchanged appearance, she clung to her newly found resolve: Somehow, she would make it work out.

Retrieving one of the three worn suitcases that contained everything she owned, Andrea carried it upstairs, and discovered that one thing *had* changed. Her room—the room that had been her only retreat after her father left and her mother sank deeper and deeper into her own strange version of religion; the room that she simply assumed would be waiting for her, welcoming her even if her mother did not—was no longer hers. Her cousin Rebecca was living in it—Rebecca's clothes in the closet; Rebecca's slippers by the side of the bed; her raggedy teddy bear perched on the pillow. The knowledge stung her sharply. Her mother had cut her out of the house as thoroughly as she'd cut her father out twenty-five years before. The wound was almost as painful as Gary's betrayal had been, and for a moment a blinding jealousy seized her. Then reason returned. None of her problems, after all, were Rebecca's fault. She certainly couldn't ask Rebecca to disrupt her life just because she had messed up her own.

With renewed determination, Andrea went back downstairs and into the room next to the dining room. Small, little more than an alcove, really, it could be closed off with a pair of pocket doors, and still contained the daybed Andrea remembered her mother had always used for naps whenever she felt too tired to climb the stairs to her own room. At least she wouldn't be in anyone's way, she thought, and she didn't need much room anyway. Opening one of her suitcases, Andrea began hanging her clothes in the room's single, tiny closet.

"What do you think you're doing?"

Her mother's voice, even harsher than she remembered it, cut through her reverie. Andrea froze, the blouse she'd been about to hang up clutched to her chest.

She wanted to say, *Aren't you glad to see me? Don't you want to know why I've come home? Don't you want to give me a hug and ask me why I look so sad?* But all she could manage was, "I—I was just putting my clothes away, Mother."

"Down here?" Martha asked, her face hardening and her lips compressing into a tight line of disapproval.

Andrea glanced nervously around the room as if the walls might offer some clue to the reason for her mother's objection.

"If you think I'm going to allow you to live down here where you can come and go at any hour of the day or night with anyone you choose, you are very wrong. Do you think I'm going to tolerate your sins right here in my house?"

"Mother, I'm not going to—"

"You will sleep in your old room, next to mine," Martha decreed. She glanced around the little room. "There's no reason why Rebecca can't use this one."

"But Mother, that's not fair! Rebecca's been using my old room for years. She shouldn't have to move now!"

Martha glared at her daughter. "Keep a respectful tongue in your head, child. 'Honor thy mother,' " she quoted. "I know the Commandments mean nothing to you, but as long as you are under my roof, you will live by them. Do you understand?"

Andrea hesitated, then nodded. But as she began removing clothing from the closet, she wondered how she was going to tell her mother about her pregnancy. Well, there wasn't really any reason to tell her right now. After all, it wasn't as if she was showing yet. Maybe she'd just wait and—

No!

That was how she'd lived her life for way too many years already, letting herself drift along, thinking that everything would work itself out. But that was over. From now on she was going to face things squarely, and deal with them. Otherwise, she'd never have a life at all.

"There's something I have to tell you, Mother," she said. Martha's eyes narrowed to suspicious slits, and though Andrea wanted to run from the accusing glare, she made herself keep her gaze firmly on her mother's face. "Gary . . . the man I've been living with, the one I thought would marry me . . . He left me. And—he fired me from my job." She hesitated, willing herself not to burst into tears. Taking a deep breath and deciding that if her mother was going to throw her out, she might as well get it over with now, she said in a rush, "I'm pregnant too."

For what seemed an eternity, Martha Ward said nothing. As the seconds ticked interminably by, Andrea wondered if her mother was, indeed, going to banish her from the house.

Finally, Martha spoke. "You will pray for forgiveness. When the child is born, we'll find a family that will take care of it. Then I shall decide what you will do next."

Andrea took another deep breath. "I already told you what I'm going to do next, Mother. I'm going to get a job, and I'm going to go back to school."

"While you're pregnant?" Martha demanded. "I don't see how—"

Andrea decided to finish what she'd begun before she lost her nerve. "I'm not sure if I'm going to stay pregnant, Mother," she said. "But whatever I decide, it's going to be my decision, not yours."

Martha Ward could barely contain her fury. How dare Andrea speak to her this way? How dare she live in sin with a man who was married to another woman, then bring the fruits of her transgressions into Martha's own home?

Martha knew what she should do: she should cast Andrea out now, cast her out of her home lest her own immortal soul be put at risk.

But then she hesitated, remembering something she'd read recently.

It was the sin she was commanded to hate, not the sinner.

In a flash of insight, she understood.

She was being tested!

Andrea had been sent back to her as a test of her faith.

Her cross to bear.

She must not cast Andrea out. Instead, no matter how deeply her wayward child offended her, she must turn the other cheek and lead her prodigal daughter back onto the path of righteousness.

Reading her mother's silence as assent for her to stay in the house, Andrea Ward picked up her suitcases and started up the stairs to the room in which she'd grown up.

Martha Ward entered her chapel and fell to her knees. Her lips moving silently, she prayed for guidance on how best to cleanse her daughter's soul.

Chapter 3

A cold drizzle was falling by the time Oliver and Rebecca got back to the *Chronicle* office. Oliver insisted on driving Rebecca home.

"You don't have to do that," she protested. "It's way out of your way. I can walk."

"Of course you *can*," Oliver told her. "But you won't. And it won't take more than a couple of minutes anyway." He fixed her with a mock glare. "Don't argue with me."

"I'm sorry," Rebecca said so quickly that Oliver immediately knew she hadn't realized he was joking. "I didn't mean—"

"No, *I'm* sorry," Oliver immediately cut in, opening the door to the Volvo for her. "You can argue with me all you want, Rebecca. About anything. But I'm still going to drive you home." This time he made certain his words were accompanied by a smile, and found himself inordinately pleased when Rebecca smiled back at him.

"I don't always get the joke, do I?" she asked as he slid behind the wheel.

"Maybe I don't make it clear enough when I'm kidding," he replied.

Rebecca shook her head. "No, it's me. I know everyone in town thinks I'm strange, but ever since the accident, I just don't seem to get things right away the way other people do."

"I don't think you're strange at all, Rebecca," Oliver

told her. Then he grinned. "But what do I know? Everybody thinks things about me too."

"No they don't."

"Sure they do. They just don't say anything to my face, that's all." Oliver pulled the Volvo up behind an old Toyota that was parked in the driveway of Martha Ward's house. "Looks like Andrea must have arrived. Do you think I should come in and say hello?"

Rebecca glanced worriedly toward the house. "Aunt Martha wouldn't like that. She—" Feeling suddenly flustered, Rebecca left the sentence uncompleted, but Oliver finished it for her.

"Is it just me she disapproves of, or is it any man at all?"

Flushing scarlet, Rebecca stared at her hands, which were kneading the brown paper bag in which Janice Anderson had put the cigarette lighter. "It's anyone," she said. "Aunt Martha doesn't trust men."

Oliver reached out and gently turned Rebecca's head so she couldn't help but look at him. "Don't believe everything Aunt Martha says," he told her. "I won't hurt you, Rebecca. I couldn't."

For a moment he thought Rebecca was going to say something, or maybe even burst into tears, but then she quickly got out of the car and hurried up the walk to the porch. At the door, she turned, hesitated, then waved to him. As he drove away, Oliver felt an overwhelming sense of relief that she hadn't gone into the house without looking back at all.

And that, he realized, told him something.

It told him that, despite his better judgment, despite telling himself that his affection for her was nothing more than friendly concern, he was falling in love with Rebecca Morrison.

How, he wondered, was he going to deal with that?

More important, how was she?

* * *

Rebecca closed the front door behind her, trading the gloom of the late afternoon for the gloom inside the house. She was about to call out to her cousin, but before Andrea's name could even form on her lips, she heard the insistent tones of the Gregorian chants that invariably accompanied her aunt's prayer sessions in the chapel. Moving quietly enough not to be heard over the music, Rebecca searched the lower floor of the house, but found no sign of Andrea. Then she realized where her cousin must be: in the chapel, praying with her mother.

But a minute later, as she was about to open the door to her room on the second floor, Rebecca stopped. She could hear something—a muffled sound like someone crying—and it was coming from inside her room. She hesitated, wondering what she should do.

It had to be Andrea, of course. But what was Andrea doing in her room? And then she remembered. The room used to be her cousin's, and Andrea had certainly expected to find it waiting for her.

Gently, Rebecca tapped at the door, but heard no response. She tapped again, a little louder this time. "Andrea? Can I come in?"

Now there was a distant sniffle, then Andrea's voice. "It's okay, Rebecca. It's not locked."

Turning the knob, Rebecca pushed the door open. Andrea was sitting on the bed, three suitcases spilling their contents on the floor around her feet. Her cheeks were streaked with tears, and she clutched a crumpled tissue in her hand.

Andrea looked thinner than Rebecca remembered her being, and tired. "Andrea?" she whispered. "You look—"

Terrible. She'd been about to say "You look terrible." But for once, instead of blurting out whatever came into her mind, Rebecca caught herself. But it was as if Andrea had read her mind.

"I look awful, don't I, Rebecca?"

Rebecca nodded automatically, and the tiniest trace of a smile played around Andrea's lips.

"I figured," her cousin said. "Apparently, I look too awful for Mom even to give me a hug. Or maybe she's just not very glad to see me."

"Oh, no!" Rebecca exclaimed. She hurried to the bed, dropped her purse and the paper bag onto it, and wrapped her arms around her cousin, then stood back and said, "You look fine! Aunt Martha doesn't hug anyone. And I'm sure she's glad to see you. She's just—"

Miraculously, Rebecca once again managed to censor herself, but once again Andrea had no trouble finishing the thought for her.

"Still crazy, right?" Her smile faded and she seemed to deflate. "I shouldn't have come back here, should I? Now it's not only going to be my life I mess up, but yours too."

Rebecca slipped her arm around her cousin in a quick hug. "You're not messing up my life. Why would you say that? I'm *glad* you came home."

"Then you haven't talked to my mother yet. She says if I stay here, I have to be in this room. She says you have to move into the room behind the dining room. Look, I feel really terrible about it. If you want me to, I'll go find somewhere else—"

"No!" Rebecca interrupted, holding a finger to Andrea's lips to silence her. "This is your home, and this was your room, and you should have it. And I really am glad you're here." She picked up the brown bag, now crumpled and sodden from the rain, and thrust it into Andrea's hands. "Look—I even bought you a present."

Andrea hesitated, and Rebecca had the strangest feeling that for some reason her cousin didn't feel she deserved whatever gift might be inside the bag.

"Please take it," Rebecca said softly. "It isn't much, but I thought you might like it. And if you don't, you don't have to keep it."

Now Andrea's eyes were shining with tears. "It isn't that at all, Rebecca. It's just—" She struggled for a moment, but couldn't hold the tears back. "Nobody's given me a present for so long that I forgot what it feels like. And I don't have anything for you. I—"

"Just open it," Rebecca begged. "Please?"

Blowing her nose into the crumpled Kleenex once more, Andrea finally opened the bag and took out the tissue-wrapped object inside. Stripping the paper away, she gazed uncomprehendingly at the gilded dragon. "I—I don't understand," she stammered. "What is it?"

Instead of telling her, Rebecca took the dragon from her cousin's hands and squeezed its neck. *Click!* And a tongue of fire shot from its mouth. Andrea laughed.

"I love it!" she said, taking the lighter back from Rebecca and trying it herself. "Where did you ever find it? It's wonderful!" Rummaging in her purse, she found a package of cigarettes at the bottom, pulled one out, and lit it from the dragon's mouth. "Now if anyone says I have dragon breath, at least they'll be right!"

"You mean you really like it?" Rebecca asked. "It's all right?"

"It's perfect," Andrea assured her. Then she glanced around. "Now I feel even worse about taking your room."

"It's not my room," Rebecca reminded her. "It's yours. And the one downstairs is fine for me. I don't need much. I'll bet I don't have nearly as many clothes as you, and I won't have to listen to Aunt Martha snore anymore." She instantly clapped her hands over her mouth as she realized she'd once more spoken without thinking, but Andrea only laughed again.

"Is it really bad?"

Rebecca nodded. "Sometimes I have to wear earplugs in order to sleep."

"Oh, Lord," Andrea moaned, flopping back onto the bed. "Maybe I'm actually doing you a favor after all."

She sat up again, then held the pack of cigarettes out to Rebecca. "Want one?"

Rebecca shook her head. "Smoking's not good for you."

Andrea laughed, but this time the sound was bitter. "Life hasn't been very good for me. No job, no husband, no place to live, and pregnant. So where's the good part?"

"You're having a baby?" Rebecca asked. "But that's wonderful, Andrea. Babies are always good, aren't they?" Then her eyes fell on the cigarette from which Andrea was inhaling deeply. "But now you really shouldn't smoke," she went on. "It's really bad for the baby."

The last faint feeling of optimism that the gift had brought to Andrea dropped away. "What the hell would you know about it?" she asked. Then, unwilling to witness the pain her words inflicted on Rebecca, she stood up and went to the window, gazing out at the dark, rainy afternoon.

Rebecca, stinging from Andrea's rebuff, went to the door. Hand on the knob, she turned back, hopefully, but when Andrea made no move even to look at her, she shook her head. "I'm sorry," she said. "I didn't mean to upset you. I just—well, I just say things, that's all. I'm really sorry."

"Just leave me alone, Rebecca. Okay?"

A moment later Andrea heard the door open and close, and knew that she was once again alone in the room. She went back to the bed, dropped down onto it once more, and picked up the lighter.

Clicking it on and off, she watched the dragon's flaming tongue flick in and out of its gilded mouth. As the flame flared then died away, flared and died once more, she thought about the baby growing in her womb.

Then, with a sharp *click* that made the dragon spit its flame again, she made up her mind what she was going to do.

Chapter 4

Martha Ward left her house at dawn the next morning. She hadn't slept well, which she always took as a sign that her soul was troubled. This morning, her private prayer session in her own chapel wouldn't be enough. Dressed in the dark blue suit she invariably wore to church, and with her hat and veil pinned carefully in place, she used her key to bolt the front door. Both Rebecca and Andrea were asleep inside the house, and though she was well aware that both of them were already steeped in sin, she was always mindful that there were men in Blackstone—just as there were men everywhere—whose hearts were filled with lust.

Satisfied that the door was firmly locked, she left the porch, buttoned her coat to her chin as the sharp wind cut into her, then made her way down Harvard Street. Her feet, misshapen from the arthritis that had been one of her crosses for the last twenty years, were hurting badly by the time she'd gone a block, but she ignored the pain, silently repeating her rosary. This morning she was saying St. Benedict's—one of her favorite rosaries—and the rhythms of the Latin words eased her pain slightly. If her Savior had been able to bear His cross through the streets of Jerusalem with graceful dignity, surely she could carry the pain of her arthritis with dignified grace. When Charles VanDeventer stopped to offer her a ride, she barely acknowledged him before turning her head firmly away from temptation.

32

When she arrived at the Catholic church on the town square, she noted with satisfaction that the door was already unlocked despite the early hour. Indeed, since Monsignor Vernon had come to Blackstone several years ago, seven o'clock mass was celebrated daily. Though she well knew that there were those in town who felt that the monsignor's Catholicism was out of step with their own, Martha Ward was not among them. From the day he arrived—from some small town out in Washington State, she recalled—Martha knew she'd found a kindred spirit. "I always leave the church open for prayer," he'd told her, "and I'll always be available to hear your confession." Not that Martha had much to confess. She made it a point to live a life of virtue. Still, she often found it comforting to talk to Monsignor.

Inside the church, Martha dipped her fingers in the font of holy water, genuflected, then walked slowly down the aisle, her eyes fixed on the face of the crucified Christ that loomed above the altar. Genuflecting again, she slipped into the first pew, dropped to her knees and began the first of her prayers. A few minutes later, catching a glimpse of movement out of the corner of her eye, she knew that Monsignor Vernon was in the confessional, waiting for her.

"Something is preying on you this morning," the priest said softly when Martha's confession was done and he'd handed down her penance, then absolved her. "I can feel that your heart is heavy."

Martha sat silently for a few seconds, her fingers working at her beads, hesitant to reveal her shame. But what choice had she? "It's my daughter," she whispered, her voice quavering. "She is pregnant, Father. But she isn't married." Did she hear a shocked gasp? She was almost certain she did.

She clutched the beads more tightly.

"You must pray," the priest said, his voice low but distinct. "Your daughter has committed a mortal sin, and you must pray for her. Pray for her to see the error of her ways. Pray for her to turn away from sin and find her way back to the Church. Pray for her to find her way into the arms of the Lord so her baby may be saved."

Martha waited, but no other words came to her from the other side of the screen. When she finally left the confessional, the church was once again empty, except for her. Returning to the pew, she dropped to her knees.

The words she'd heard in the confessional echoed in her mind.

Pray for her to find her way into the arms of the Lord so her baby may be saved.

Over and over again the monsignor's resonant voice echoed in her mind, until the words took on the cadence of a chant that resounded louder and louder, filling the entire church and penetrating to the very core of her being.

It was as if she'd been spoken to by the Lord Himself. Martha Ward felt transfigured.

The Lord would show her the way.

Andrea would be saved.

As soon as she was wide enough awake to remember where she was and why she was there, Andrea Ward felt her good intentions of the previous day evaporate. She reached over to the nightstand, felt for her cigarettes, and lit one with the dragon's head lighter her cousin had given her yesterday afternoon. Sucking the first puff of smoke deep into her lungs, she choked, then fell victim to a fit of coughing. When the coughing finally subsided, she dropped back onto the single thin pillow that had been allotted to the bed—her mother had never believed that more than one could possibly be necessary—and wondered why she'd bothered to wake up at all.

Nothing had changed overnight. She was still pregnant, still jobless, and Gary had still run out on her. But now she was back home in Blackstone, and her mother was condemning her for her sins, and Rebecca—

Rebecca! Christ! Though it was true that her cousin had tried to be nice to her, so what? Since her accident, Rebecca was even more useless than she'd been before, if that was possible. Sweet, maybe, but useless. Which meant Rebecca wasn't going to be any good to her at all.

Stop it! Andrea commanded herself. None of this is Rebecca's fault. You got yourself into this mess, so now it's up to you to get yourself out of it!

Stubbing the cigarette out in the soap dish she'd commandeered from the bathroom to serve as an ashtray, Andrea slid off the bed, only to feel a wave of nausea break over her as she stood. Running to the bathroom, she made it just in time to throw up into the toilet. Groping, she found the handle on the side of the tank and flushed the bowl, but as she started to get to her feet, her stomach recoiled again, a foul mixture of acid and bile rising in her throat, and she sank again to her knees. Whimpering, she stayed crouched on the floor waiting for the nausea to pass, and after retching two more times, decided to risk standing up once again. She was turning on the water to rinse the residue of vomit from her mouth when she heard a tapping at the door, immediately followed by Rebecca's voice.

"Are you all right, Andrea? Can I help?"

"No one can help," Andrea groaned. "Just go away, okay?"

There was a silence, followed by the sound of her cousin's footsteps retreating back toward the staircase. She stared at herself in the mirror. Her eyes were bloodshot, and her hair, darkening badly at the roots, lay against her scalp in a limp, oily tangle. To her own eye, she looked at least ten years older than she was. She looked worn. She looked the way she felt. Hopeless.

How on earth would she manage to keep all the promises she'd made yesterday?

Andrea went back to her room, put on the same blouse and faded jeans she'd worn the day before, and finally went downstairs. She found Rebecca in the kitchen. Two places were set at the table. As Andrea sank down into one of the chairs, Rebecca put a glass of orange juice in front of her, and a plate containing an English muffin thickly coated with butter and bright orange marmalade.

Just the sight of it made Andrea's stomach churn again. "All I want is a cup of coffee," she pleaded.

The welcoming smile on Rebecca's face faded into a look of uncertainty. "Is that good for the baby? I think I read—"

Andrea glared at her cousin. "I have news for you," she said. "I don't give a good goddamn what you *read*." As Rebecca's eyes glistened with tears, Andrea felt a twinge of guilt. "Look, I'm sorry, okay? But it hasn't been a great morning so far. I didn't sleep more than an hour, and then I started puking my brains out. Right now my life isn't going real well, you know? Anyway, I'm sorry I snapped at you."

"It's all right." Rebecca picked up the plate and glass and moved them to the counter, then poured her cousin a cup of coffee.

"Where's Mother?" Andrea asked. "She can't be asleep—she always thought being in bed after six was some kind of sin."

"Sometimes she goes to church," Rebecca explained. "Especially when she's worried about something."

Andrea rolled her eyes. "Well, I think we can both guess what she's praying about this morning, huh? What'll you bet she starts in on me the minute she gets home?"

"Aunt Martha's been good to me," Rebecca said. "And she only wants what's best for you too. She worries about you all the time."

"Worries about *me*?" Andrea cried, her voice mocking. Her hands shaking with sudden anger, she lit another cigarette. "Let me tell you something, Rebecca. Mother never worried about anyone in her whole life. All she worries about is who's sinning, and whether she's going to Heaven or not. Well, I have a news flash for her too—if Heaven is where nice, loving mothers go, then it's way too late for her already!"

Rebecca recoiled from Andrea's venom. "She's not that bad."

"Isn't she?" Andrea shot back. "Let me show you something." Standing so abruptly she nearly toppled her chair, Andrea left the kitchen and walked quickly through the house until she came to the closed doors to the room that had once been her father's den. Shoving the doors open, she stepped inside. "Did you know this is where I grew up?" she asked. Using the dragon's head, she began lighting the candles lined up on her mother's small altar, then lit the ones that stood beneath the icons of the Holy Mother and half a dozen saints.

"This is the way it always was, Rebecca," she said as the dark room began to glow with the shadowy light of the shimmering candle flames. "Ever since I was a little girl, this is how it was. I had to come in here and pray every morning, and every day after school, and every night before I went to bed. And you know what, Rebecca? I never even got to see what it looked like in real light. Well, let's find out, shall we?"

Crossing the room first to the window on the left of the altar, then to the one on the right, Andrea pulled the heavy drapes back. As the bright daylight washed away the candles' glow, the room seemed to change. The walls—once painted white—were grimy with the soot of the thousands of candles that had been burned in the chapel, and the upholstery on the prie-dieu was revealed to be stained and threadbare. The statues of the saints, their colors showing garishly in the daylight, were as grime-streaked as the walls. "Why wouldn't I have gotten out of here as soon as I could? What kind of woman would raise a child in a place like this?"

"But she loves you—" Rebecca began.

Andrea didn't let her finish. "It wasn't love, Rebecca! It was insanity. Don't you get it? She's nuts. Or isn't it just her anymore? Has she gotten to you too now? Or was it the accident? Did it make you so stupid you can't see what she's like? God! Why did I come back here?" Throwing her cigarette onto the carpet, she ground it out with her heel, then stormed out of the room, and raced up the stairs.

Rebecca picked up the cigarette butt and did her best to scratch the burned surface of the carpet away, then hurriedly pulled the drapes, plunging the room once more into the gloom that hid its flaws. Blowing out the candles, she pulled the chapel door closed just as Andrea reappeared at the foot of the stairs, wearing a coat and clutching the keys to her car in her hand.

"Where are you going?" Rebecca asked.

Andrea's eyes fixed darkly on her for a brief second. "Why would you care?" she demanded. Then, before Rebecca could reply, she was gone.

An hour later Rebecca had cleaned up the kitchen, her room next to the dining room, and Andrea's room too. She'd been on her way downstairs to have a last cup of coffee before going to work, but when she heard the music in the chapel begin and realized her aunt was back from church, she changed her mind and started down Harvard Street toward the library instead. She was still half an hour early, though, and since Germaine Wagner had never given her a key to the library, she decided to go over to the Red Hen and have her cup of coffee there. She was just pulling the door to the diner open when she heard a car horn honk and turned to see Oliver Metcalf nosing his car into an empty slot in front of the movie theater next to the diner.

"If you sit with me, I'll pay," Oliver said after he'd parked and approached her.

"You don't have to do that," Rebecca replied. "I have my own money, you know."

"Great," Oliver said, holding the diner's door open. "Then you can pay. How's that?"

"That would be nice," Rebecca told him. "Everybody's always offering to pay for me, like I'm still a little girl. And it's stupid, since I'm almost thirty."

Oliver feigned shock. "I had no idea," he said. "If you're that old, then you can buy me a doughnut too." They settled onto a pair of stools at the counter, and Oliver smiled at her. "How did Andrea like her present?"

Rebecca's brow furrowed. "I'm not sure," she replied. "I thought she liked it when I gave it to her last night, but this morning she just seemed to be mad about everything." As Oliver listened, she recounted everything that had happened since she'd seen him yesterday. "I just don't understand," she finished a few minutes later. "If she hates Aunt Martha so much and thinks she's crazy, why did she come home?"

"It doesn't sound like she had anyplace else to go," Oliver replied. "And if I were you, I wouldn't worry too much about what happened this morning. She's had a bad time, and it must seem to her like her life is nothing but problems. You just happened to be there when she had to blow off some steam, that's all."

Rebecca glanced at Oliver, but her gaze quickly shifted away. "But she sounded like she really meant it when she said I was so stupid I can't see what Aunt Martha's like." She was silent for a second, and then, still not looking at Oliver, asked, "Is it true, Oliver? Am I stupid?"

As he had in the car the day before, Oliver turned Rebecca's face toward him so she had no choice but to look at him. "Of course it's not true, Rebecca," he said, his voice gentle. "And I don't think Andrea meant it. She was just upset, and people say things they don't mean when they're upset. So the best thing for you to do is just forget it." Then, acting on an impulse before letting himself think about it, he leaned forward and kissed her softly on the lips. "You're not stupid," he whispered into her ear. "You're a wonderful, lovely woman, and I love you very much." Then, feeling his face flush with embarrassment, he quickly stood and looked at his watch. "I'm late," he said. Dropping some money on the counter, and feeling every eye in the diner watching him, he hurried out the door.

✳

Chapter 5

Oliver pulled his car into the parking lot of the white building that had housed Blackstone Memorial Hospital for the last twenty years. There were only three beds, and even they were rarely used: anyone who needed long-term care went either up to Manchester or down to Boston. For the last few months, though, the hospital had been busier than usual; first with Elizabeth McGuire's tragic miscarriage, then with taking care of Madeline Hartwick. Jules Hartwick's body had been taken first to Blackstone Memorial too, but even as the ambulance carried it downhill, everyone knew it was only going there as a matter of legal formality.

Oliver was still haunted by that terrible night when he'd found Jules on the steps of the Asylum and seen him plunge the knife deep into his own belly. It seemed to Oliver as if his headaches had been getting even worse lately, and yesterday, when his hand reflexively jerked away from the cigarette lighter Rebecca had bought for Andrea at the flea market, he'd been far more frightened than he let on.

Perhaps, if he hadn't been suffering from the blinding headaches, he might not have been so frightened by the false message of searing heat that his involuntary nervous system had received. But in combination with the headaches, an idea had begun forming in his mind, and though he told himself it was ridiculous, he hadn't been able to shake it all night long.

Brain tumor.

How else to explain the sudden onset of the unbearable migraines—when he'd rarely suffered from even mild headaches his whole life? How else to account for the odd flashes of vision—hallucinations—that seemed to accompany the hammering pain, though he could never quite recall their content after the headache passed. And yesterday . . . When he touched the lighter, he hadn't had a headache. Yet he could still clearly remember the searing heat he'd felt in the brief instant when his fingers first touched the object.

The searing heat that—impossibly—was no longer there a second later, when Rebecca put the lighter into his hand.

Well, Phil Margolis would undoubtedly have an answer for him. Getting out of the Volvo, Oliver went into the hospital.

"All this does is take a picture of your brain," Dr. Margolis explained. The CAT scanner sat in a small room that had been renovated specifically to house it after the doctor succeeded in putting together enough funds to buy the used machine five years ago. Serving not only Blackstone, but half a dozen other towns, the scanner had brought in enough money to allow the tiny hospital to operate in the black for the first time in its history. "Lie down on the table, and I'll strap you in."

"Do you have to?" Oliver asked. The moment he'd stepped into the room, he felt a wave of panic begin to build inside him. Now, his eyes fixed on the heavy nylon restraining straps, and his palms went suddenly clammy.

"I have to hold you immobile," Margolis explained. "Any movement of your head, and the images will be spoiled. It's easiest if you're strapped down."

Oliver hesitated, wondering where the panic was coming from. He'd never been claustrophobic—at least he didn't think he had—but for some reason the idea of being strapped to the bed terrified him. But why? It couldn't have anything to do with Phil Margolis—he'd known the doctor for years.

Could it be he was just frightened of what the CAT scan might show? But that was ridiculous—if there was something wrong with him, he wanted to know about it! "All right," he said, lying down on the table. Fists clenched, he shut his eyes and steeled himself against the fear that instantly gripped him as the doctor began fastening the straps that would hold him immobile. His heart raced; he could feel the sweat on his palms.

"You okay, Oliver?" the doctor asked.

"Fine." But he wasn't fine; he wasn't fine at all. A terrible fear was overtaking him, an unreasoning terror.

"Okay, we're all set," Phil Margolis told him. He stepped out of the room, and a moment later the machine came to life, the scanner starting to move down over his head as it began taking thousands of pictures from every possible angle, which a computer would then knit together to form a perfect image of his brain.

And anything that might be growing inside it.

Then it happened.

With no warning at all, a blinding pain slashed through Oliver's head, and the room seemed to fill with a brilliant white light that faded to utter blackness in an instant. And then, out of the blackness, an image appeared.

The boy is in a small room, staring at a table to which heavy leather straps are attached. The man, looming above him, is waiting impatiently for the boy to get onto the table. In his hand, the man holds something.

Something the boy has seen before.

Something that terrifies him.

Instead of getting on the table, the boy retreats to cower in a corner of the room.

As the man raises the object, with two shining

metal studs protruding from a long tube at one end, the boy whimpers, already anticipating the pain to come.

As the man advances toward the boy, the child, screaming now, starts to run. The man's large, muscled arm reaches out—

"That's it," Philip Margolis said as he came back into the room. He unfastened the straps that held Oliver to the table. "That wasn't so terrible, was it?"

Oliver hesitated. The fact was, he couldn't really remember much of the scan at all. There had been a moment of panic, but then . . .

What?

A headache? One of the strange hallucinations?

Something—some kind of vague memory—was flitting about the edges of his consciousness, but as he reached out for it, trying to grasp it, the memory slipped away.

Oliver managed a grin as he sat up, the straps having released their grip. "Not so bad," he agreed. "Not so bad at all."

Chapter 6

*A*ndrea drove slowly, searching for the impossible: an empty parking spot in Boston. She'd already passed the red brick building three times, twice going this direction, once the other. Should she try the other side again, or give up hoping to find a spot within a few steps of the building, and try one of the side streets?

Or should she just turn around and drive back to Blackstone?

She rejected the last idea immediately. She'd thought it all through too many times to back out now. If she didn't go through with it now, she never would. Her mother would start in on her, and this time there would be no escape. Sooner or later she'd give in. And whatever Martha decided, it wouldn't be good for her, and it wouldn't be good for the baby.

It would be good only for Martha Ward, who would then spend the next few years exacting emotional payment for having "gotten you out of that mess, even though I had nothing to do with getting you into it!" A three-way bank shot, the kind Andrea knew her mother loved best, leaving Andrea feeling guilty, grateful, and indebted, all at the same time.

But not this time. This time Andrea was going to take care of it—take charge of her own life. Her mind made up, she turned off onto a side street, resuming her search for a parking spot. She finally found one three blocks from her destination, pulled into it, and automatically locked the rusting Toyota, even though she suspected it was worth more stolen than not. Hunched against the cold drizzle that had begun an hour before, Andrea trudged back toward the clinic, her steps heavy, her eyes fixed on the pavement in front of her.

The doctor's office was on the third floor. To Andrea's surprise, the door was unlocked. There were several women in the waiting room. Only one, a neatly dressed Asian woman several years younger than she, glanced up when she came in. The woman smiled briefly, then quickly lowered her eyes again to the magazine she was leafing through. A white-coated receptionist behind a glass partition looked up and said to Andrea, "May I help you?"

Andrea hesitated. There was still time to change her mind, still time to turn around and just walk out.

But then what?

Then, nothing.

No school, no decent job, no life.

Ever.

"I was wondering if Dr. Randall has an opening today," she asked.

The nurse glanced down at the appointment calendar that was spread open before her. "Can you come back at two?"

Andrea nodded, gave the nurse her name, then filled out a medical history form, and filled in her MasterCard number, uttering a silent prayer that Gary had neither canceled the card nor run it past its credit limit. The first was doubtful; the second not at all unlikely. Leaving the office, she went back to the street, spotted a Starbucks half a block down on the other side, and settled in for the long wait.

When she returned to the office at exactly two that afternoon, the waiting room was empty. "Right on time," the nurse said, smiling at her again. She opened the inner door and led Andrea into the doctor's office, where a man of about forty, with a blond crew cut, the build of a football player, and a ruggedly handsome face rose and offered her his hand.

"I'm Bob Randall."

As Andrea sank into the chair opposite the doctor, he reached for the forms she'd filled out, and she saw the gold wedding band on his finger. Damn.

"Do you want to talk about this?" Randall asked.

Andrea groaned to herself. Now what? Was she going to have to explain herself to the doctor too? What business was it of his? The operation was perfectly legal— hundreds of women had it every day, and thousands more, she believed, should have.

The doctor seemed to read her mind. "I don't mean about having the abortion," he said. "I just mean about the procedure itself."

"You mean you're not going to guilt-trip me?" Andrea asked.

Randall shrugged. "It's your life, and your body, and nobody but you has the right to tell you what to do with it. You're old enough to know what you're doing, and if you're as healthy as you say you are, there shouldn't be any problems. You'll be out of here in little more than an hour."

For just a moment, Andrea hesitated. Even though she'd been told Dr. Randall wouldn't lecture her, she hadn't really believed it.

But this was it.

No questions, no arguments.

She nodded her head. "Let's do it."

The doctor took her into another room, left her alone while she changed into a hospital gown, and then came back, this time with the nurse. He checked Andrea's blood pressure and pulse, her respiration and reflexes. He listened to her chest, palpated her stomach, then told her to stretch out on her back and put her feet in stirrups.

"Last chance to change your mind," he told her.

"Go ahead," Andrea said. "Let's just get it over with."

Fifteen minutes later it was all over. There had been surprisingly little discomfort; the worst had been when he'd dilated her cervix, but even that hadn't hurt badly. "Is that it?" she asked as the nurse began cleaning up the small operating room.

"That's all there is," the doctor replied. "I'd like you to lie down and relax for half an hour or so, and then I'll take a look to make sure there aren't any problems, but I can't really imagine that there are going to be any. It's a very simple procedure, and I know what I'm doing."

Forty minutes later Andrea was dressed and back out on the street. It had stopped drizzling. The first thing she did when she was out of the brick building in which she'd at least solved the worst of her problems was to reach into her purse and pull out a cigarette.

A cigarette, and the lighter that Rebecca had given her yesterday.

She squeezed the trigger concealed in the dragon's throat, lit the cigarette, and sucked the smoke deep into her lungs, at last feeling a loosening of the tension she'd had all day.

Rebecca.

She'd have to apologize to Rebecca for what she'd said this morning.

And thank her for the lighter too. She was still holding it in her hand, and now, as the sun broke through the clouds overhead, it glinted brightly. She held it up, gazed at its red eyes, and once again squeezed its neck.

Click. Its flaming tongue appeared, flickering in the light breeze.

Andrea gazed at the lighter for a long time. Its red eyes glinted at her with a fiery light that seemed to come, not from the sun, but from deep within the dragon's golden body. Glowing crimson, the eyes held her mesmerized. Then, almost unaware of what she was doing, she held her other hand up too.

Very slowly she moved her hand toward the dragon's fiery tongue.

When the flame touched her skin, it didn't hurt.

It didn't hurt at all.

✳

Chapter 7

*D*usk had fallen as Andrea pulled up in front of her mother's house. In all the other houses on the block, except for the Hartwicks' next door, windows were already glowing with light, and thin curtains revealed glimpses of warm, inviting interiors. Only her mother's house was dark; save for the dim porch light that might provide a measure of safety to someone climbing the front steps, but offered no real welcome, the house appeared to be deserted. Yet Andrea was certain her mother was at home. She could almost feel Martha's unforgiving presence inside, almost see her kneeling on the prie-dieu, her fingers clicking through her rosary beads while her lips formed the words, *Hail Mary, Mother of God. Pray for us now and in the hour of . . .* Except that it would be the Ave Maria her mother was reciting, repeating the prayer over and over again in the original Latin, understanding no more of the prayers she uttered than she understood the daughter she'd raised.

Andrea shut off the car's engine, but instead of getting out of the Toyota, she reached into her purse, found her cigarettes, and used the dragon to light one. As she sat in the car, smoking her cigarette, she idly flicked the lighter on and off, watching the tongue of flame flare quickly, then die away. The cigarette was only half smoked when she was startled by a rap on the glass and glanced over to see Rebecca peering worriedly through the curbside window.

"Andrea? Are you all right?"

Stubbing the cigarette out in the car's ashtray, Andrea got out. "I'm okay, I guess." She sighed, knowing she wasn't okay at all. The first terrible doubt about what she'd done had set in even before she'd gotten back in her car. Over and over, she'd tried to convince herself that she'd done the right thing, but she still hadn't been able to rid herself of the nagging feeling that she could have coped with the situation another way. Surely she could have found some kind of job: pregnant women worked all the time—lots of them right up until a week or so before they were ready to deliver. And after the baby was born, there would have been lots of options. She could have put the baby up for adoption, or maybe even kept it and—

Stop it, she commanded herself. It's over and done with.

Rebecca was still looking at her anxiously. Andrea forced herself to smile as she came around to the curb. "Hey, it's all right," she said. "I'm going to be okay. And look, I'm sorry about this morning, okay? I mean, I was having morning sickness and feeling like a mess, and—well, you were there, so I took it all out on you. So I'm sorry. And I really like the lighter. I've been using it all day."

"But with the baby—" Rebecca began, but Andrea didn't let her finish.

"Will you stop worrying? I said everything's going to be okay. All right?" They were on the porch now, and as Rebecca opened the front door, Andrea smelled the familiar, choking scent of incense and candle smoke, and heard the drone of the recorded chanting. "She's praying, isn't she?"

Rebecca nodded. "I was just starting supper."

"I'll help." Andrea hung her coat in the closet, then followed Rebecca into the kitchen, where the table was set for two.

Rebecca, seeing Andrea's eyes fix on the two places,

reddened. "I didn't know whether you were going to be here or not," she said quickly. "I'll set another—"

"For God's sake, Rebecca, take it easy. I'll set another place." She eyed the small table at which she and her mother had eaten all their meals since her father had left, and at which, presumably, Rebecca and her mother had been eating for the last twelve years. "I have an idea. What do you say we use the dining room?"

Rebecca's eyes widened. "I don't think Aunt Martha would like that."

"Who cares what Mother would like?" Andrea countered. "What about what you and I would like? Haven't you ever wanted to eat in the dining room?" Without waiting for an answer, Andrea scooped the two place settings off the kitchen table and put them back in the cabinet to the right of the sink. "And I think we'll just use the good silver tonight too," she announced.

Half an hour later Rebecca dished the warmed-up pot roast, left over from the night before, onto the good china. Just as she and Andrea were carrying the plates in from the kitchen, the chanting from the chapel stopped abruptly and Martha Ward appeared at the end of the hall. Before her mother could say a word, Andrea spoke.

"We're eating in the dining room tonight, Mother."

"We never eat in the dining room," Martha stated.

"Well, we are tonight. The kitchen table's too small, and what's the point of having a dining room if we never use it?"

"The dining room is for company," Martha said coldly.

"Come on, Mother. When was the last time you had company?"

Martha's lips pursed in disapproval, but she said nothing until she came into the dining room and surveyed the table. Andrea had not only set it with the good silver, but had put a cloth on the table, and candles in the twin candelabra that had stood unused on the sideboard for a quarter of a century. Rebecca hovered near the door, certain that Martha was going to demand that supper be moved to the kitchen and the dining room table be cleared instantly. When her aunt finally spoke, though, the chill in her voice had softened slightly.

"Perhaps we can consider this a celebration of Andrea's homecoming," she said. The tension in the room eased slightly, and Rebecca and Andrea took their seats on opposite sides of the table as Martha settled herself into the chair at the head. "But only for tonight," she went on. "I'm sure the three of us can fit around the kitchen table perfectly comfortably. Shall we say grace?"

Martha bowed her head. Andrea winked conspiratorially at Rebecca, who quickly tilted her own head forward and clasped her hands as her aunt muttered the prayer. When Martha was done, she picked up her knife and fork, cut a piece of pot roast, and put it in her mouth. She chewed it for a long time, finally swallowed it, then fixed her eyes on her daughter. "I spoke to Monsignor Vernon this morning, Andrea."

Andrea looked at her mother guardedly. "Oh?"

"He says I must pray for you."

Andrea tensed, girding herself for the lecture she knew her mother was preparing to deliver. "I'm afraid it's a little late for that," Andrea ventured. "I haven't been as good as you about going to church."

Martha regarded her daughter sadly, as if contemplating whether it was already far too late for her to find redemption. Still, she thought, she must follow her priest's instructions. "Monsignor Vernon says I must pray that you will find a way to return to the arms of the Lord. For the sake of the baby," she added pointedly, lest Andrea mistake her purpose.

Andrea, about to put a bite of food in her mouth, slowly put down her fork, then looked directly at her mother. "If you're planning to pray for my baby," she said, "you don't need to waste your time. There isn't going to be a baby. I went back down to Boston today and had it taken care of."

Martha Ward's face paled. "Taken care of?" she repeated, her voice barely audible. "Exactly what do you mean, Andrea?"

Andrea searched her mother's face for any trace of sympathy for what she'd been going through, any hint that her mother might understand why she'd done what she had. But there was none, and suddenly the doubts she'd had about the abortion vanished as she realized the future her child would have had: Her mother would have found some way—any way—to take the baby away from her. Then the child would have grown up in this house, suffocated by her mother's fanaticism, believing that it was conceived in sin and damned for all eternity.

With a certainty proved by the unforgiving sanctimony of her mother's expression, Andrea knew she'd made the right decision.

"I mean I had an abortion this afternoon, Mother."

A stifling shroud of silence fell over the dining room as Martha and Andrea stared at each other. Finally, Martha rose from her chair and pointed an accusing finger at her daughter. "Murderess," she hissed. Then her voice rose. "Murderess! May you burn in Hell!"

Turning her back on her daughter, Martha Ward strode out of the room. Within seconds the sound of Gregorian chants swelled through the house.

"She's praying for you," Rebecca said softly.

"No she isn't," Andrea replied. "She's praying for herself. She doesn't give a damn about me."

"That isn't true," Rebecca said. "She loves you."

Now Andrea too was on her feet. "No she doesn't, Rebecca. She doesn't love anyone." Tears streaming down her cheeks, Andrea fled from the dining room.

As the house filled with the mysterious droning rhythm of the chanting, Rebecca sadly cleared the dining room table and wondered if it would ever be used again.

* * *

Rebecca wasn't certain what woke her up; indeed, at first she wasn't sure she'd fallen asleep at all. Though the doors to her small room were closed, she could still hear the music emanating from the chapel, just as it had been when she'd gone to bed. Rolling over, she glanced at the little travel alarm clock she'd brought down from Andrea's room yesterday afternoon.

Three o'clock.

Three o'clock?

She sat up in bed, wide-awake now, and for the first time noticed something else.

There was a smell in the house; not the normal sickly sweet smell of her aunt's incense, but the acrid odor of the smoke that had filled the living room the one time she'd tried to use the fireplace, only to discover that her aunt had long ago had the chimney blocked to keep the house from losing heat.

Smoke?

Getting out of bed, Rebecca pulled on her bathrobe as she went to the pocket doors that separated her sleeping room from the dining room beyond. Before the panels were even inches apart, the acrid smell grew stronger, and she choked as she drew in a breath of smoky air. Throwing the doors wide open, she ran to the foot of the stairs.

The smoke was far thicker there. She watched in horror as more of it billowed down from the floor above.

"Fire!" she yelled up the stairs. "Andrea, get out! The house is on fire!" When there was no reply, she started up the stairs, but the smoke immediately drove her back down, coughing and gasping for breath. Her mind racing, she shouted again, this time to her aunt, then ran back to the kitchen to snatch up the phone. Fumbling twice, she finally managed to punch 911 into the keypad. Dropping to the floor to avoid the smoke that was now pouring into the kitchen from the hallway, she yelled into the phone

the moment the emergency operator came on the line:
"It's Rebecca Morrison—please! Help! The house is
burning. I live at—" Suddenly, Rebecca's mind blanked,
and she felt panic rising in her. Then she heard the operator's voice.

"I already have the address," the operator told her.
"You're at 527 Harvard. The engines are on the way."

Dropping the phone, Rebecca ran out of the kitchen
and back down the hall. At the foot of the stairs she
shouted for her cousin once more, then charged through
to the other side of the house, jerking open the door to
her aunt's chapel.

All the candles were lit, and her aunt was on her knees
at the prie-dieu, her head bowed, her fingers clutching
her rosary.

"Aunt Martha!" Rebecca shouted. "The house is on
fire! We have to get out!"

Slowly, almost as if in a trance, Martha Ward turned
her head and gazed at Rebecca. "It's all right, child," she
said softly. "The Lord will look after us."

Ignoring her aunt's words, Rebecca grabbed Martha
Ward's arm and, with all her strength tugged her to her
feet, then out of the candlelit room and into the foyer.
Jerking the front door open, she shoved her aunt out onto
the porch, then stumbled after her. Rain had begun to
fall, but Rebecca ignored it as she pulled Martha off the
porch and out into the yard as sirens wailed in the night.
Rebecca looked up to the second floor, once again calling
out her cousin's name. But even as she shouted to
Andrea, she knew it might already be too late: unlike any
of the other windows in the house, Andrea's were
glowing orange from the flames that danced within.

Rebecca sank to her knees on the front lawn. Oblivious to the rain and the cold, with tears streaming down
her face, she joined her aunt in prayer.

✳

Chapter 8

*R*ebecca sat trembling in the waiting room of Blackstone Memorial. She was doing her best to answer all the questions she was being asked. Most of what had happened was still clear in her mind. She recalled waking up and smelling smoke, then calling out to her aunt and cousin to warn them that the house was burning. After that, as events started moving faster and faster, her memories were jumbled. She remembered calling 911, and getting her aunt out of the house. But then it became a blur. The fire engines began arriving, and a police car, and people had come out of the other houses. That was when they started asking her questions, but there were so many people and so many questions, she couldn't keep them sorted out. Finally, when Andrea was carried out of the house and put in the ambulance, Rebecca had begged to be allowed to go to the hospital with her.

She'd crouched on the floor of the ambulance, trying to stay out of the way of the medics, who were putting an IV in Andrea's arm. When she got her first good look at her cousin, she almost screamed out loud. Andrea's face was badly burned; her eyebrows were gone, and flesh was peeling from her cheeks and nose. The skin on her arms and shoulders was blackened, and all her hair was gone, except for a charred stubble on her blistered scalp. Though Rebecca quickly looked away, she felt a terrible hopelessness flood over her, wondering if Andrea would survive even long enough for them to get to the hospital.

But when the ambulance had finally screeched to a stop, her cousin was still breathing, and Rebecca scrambled out of the ambulance fast enough not to delay the medics. A few seconds later they pushed past her with the stretcher bearing Andrea's body, and Rebecca thought she heard a faint moan.

Rebecca had been clinging to that sound ever since, while the waiting room quickly filled with people and the questions began all over again. This time, though, it was the deputy sheriff, Steve Driver, who had put his hands on her shoulders to stop her trembling, and was gazing down intently at her.

"Is there anything else you can remember, Rebecca? Anything at all?"

She shook her head. "I've told it all."

Driver shifted his gaze to Martha Ward, who was sitting next to her niece, her rosary clutched in her fingers, her lips working as she silently recited her prayers. "What about you, Mrs. Ward? Did you hear anything? If you were awake—"

"She was praying," Rebecca said quietly. "When she prays, she never hears anything at all. She didn't even hear me when I came into the chapel to get her out of the house."

Steve Driver reached out and touched Martha's arm. "Mrs. Ward? I need to talk to you. It's really important." When Martha only kept on praying, he squeezed her arm and shook her slightly. "Mrs. Ward!"

As if jerked out of a deep sleep, Martha suddenly looked up. There was an odd, empty look in her eyes, but then her hands dropped into her lap and she shook her head sorrowfully. "It was God's will," she pronounced.

Steve Driver frowned, glanced at Rebecca, then turned his attention back to Martha. Leaning forward, he took her hands in his. "Mrs. Ward? Can you hear me?"

Martha seemed to gather herself together, taking a deep breath and straightening in the plastic chair on which she was perched. "Of course I can hear you. And I'm telling you what happened. God has punished Andrea for her sin."

The deputy's frown deepened. "Her sin?"

"She killed her child," Martha said, her voice strong now, and carrying throughout the waiting room. "And God has stricken her down."

The deputy sheriff cast a questioning glance at Rebecca.

"Andrea had an abortion," she explained. "Aunt Martha didn't approve of it, and—"

Martha drew up still straighter, and now her eyes fixed angrily on her niece. "God didn't approve," she declared. "God judges, not I. All I can do is pray for the soul of the child she murdered." Her fingers tightened once more on her beads. "We shall pray. We shall—"

Before she could finish, the door separating the waiting room from the emergency room opened and a nurse appeared. Spotting Rebecca, she hurried over and knelt down. "Your cousin's awake, and she's asking to see you," she said.

"Me?" Rebecca asked, her voice puzzled. "Shouldn't Aunt Martha—"

"It's you she's asking for, Rebecca," the nurse said.

"How is she?" Steve Driver asked, rising to his feet. "Is she going to make it?"

"We don't know," the nurse said quickly. "She has third-degree burns on most of her body." She shook her head. "She must be in terrible pain." She turned back to Rebecca. "But she's awake, and she's asking for you. It's going to be very difficult for you, but—"

"It's all right," Rebecca assured her. "It can't be nearly as bad for me as it is for Andrea."

She followed the nurse through the double doors and into the emergency treatment room. Andrea was lying on an examining table. There was a large bottle attached to the IV that the medic had put in her arm while she was still in the ambulance, and there was another tube in her nose. Dr. Margolis and two of the medics were carefully picking what looked like dead skin from Andrea's body, but as she drew closer to the bed, Rebecca realized it wasn't skin at all, but the remains of the nylon nightgown Andrea had been wearing when the fire broke out. Rebecca winced as one of the medics lifted a scrap of the material loose, taking a small patch of burned skin as well.

"I—I'm lucky," Andrea breathed, her voice barely audible. "I can't feel it yet."

Rebecca started to reach out to take her cousin's hand, stopping herself just in time. "Thank God you're still alive," Rebecca whispered. "And you're going to be all right."

She saw a barely perceptible shake of her cousin's head. "I don't think so," Andrea whispered. "I just—" She fell silent, winced as she tried to take a breath, then managed to utter a few more words. "My fault," she breathed. "Fell asleep with . . . cigarette. Dumb, huh?"

"It's all right, Andrea," Rebecca told her. "It wasn't your fault. It was an accident."

"No accident," Andrea whispered. "Mother said—"

"It doesn't matter what Aunt Martha said," Rebecca told her. "The only thing that matters is that you're alive, and you're going to get well."

For a long time Andrea said nothing, and Rebecca thought she must have gone to sleep. Then she spoke one more time. "The dragon," she breathed. "Don't let—"

Rebecca leaned forward, straining to hear what her cousin was saying. Andrea struggled, then her charred lips worked again. "M-Mother," she whispered. "Don't—" But before she could finish, the sedatives that had been added to the IV took hold and Andrea drifted into unconsciousness. She lay so still that finally Rebecca looked up at the nurse.

"What happened? Did she—"

"She's asleep," the nurse said. "If you'd like to go back to the waiting room . . ."

Rebecca shook her head, her eyes never leaving Andrea's ruined face. "Can't I stay here?" she asked. "What if she wakes up again? If I'm here, maybe she won't be so frightened."

The nurse hesitated, then indicated a chair close to the door. "Of course you can stay with her, Rebecca," she said. As Rebecca lowered herself into the chair, the nurse went back to work, helping the medics and Dr. Margolis clean the worst of Andrea's wounds and treat them with Silvadene ointment to try to prevent infection.

Rebecca, feeling utterly helpless, could only watch in silence.

Oliver Metcalf stood up and stretched, then stepped outside to suck a few breaths of morning air into his lungs. He'd been at the hospital for four hours, arriving minutes after Rebecca had been taken in to see Andrea.

He'd collected every scrap of information about the fire he could get. He and Steve Driver had come to the same conclusion. The fire had undoubtedly been an accident, caused by Andrea's habit of smoking in bed. The crew that had put the fire out had found an ashtray next to the bed, and though it was overturned, there were half a dozen sodden cigarette butts scattered around the floor in the same area. The only thing that saved Martha Ward was that she'd been praying in her downstairs chapel, and even that might not have saved her if Rebecca hadn't awakened.

"It could have been a lot worse," Driver said as he and Oliver finished comparing notes.

With nothing more that could be accomplished at the hospital, Driver had left. As the night wore on, the waiting room slowly emptied, until only Oliver and Martha Ward were still there. Though Oliver had tried several times to speak to Martha, she utterly ignored him as she concentrated on a seemingly endless repetition of her prayers. Eventually the rain stopped and the day dawned, the sun shining outside.

Half an hour before, Philip Margolis had come into the waiting room to ask Martha Ward if she wanted to see her daughter. Martha shook her head.

"I am praying for her," she said. "For her and her child both. I don't need to see her."

The doctor, nearly exhausted after hours of trying to save Andrea's life, turned away in disgust and started back to his patient. Oliver stopped him.

"How's she doing?" he asked, but even as he uttered the question, the expression on the doctor's face told him all he needed to know.

"I don't see how she can hold out much longer," Margolis said. He looked carefully at Oliver. "What about you? How are you feeling? Any more of those headaches?"

Oliver shook his head.

"Well, there's nothing in your CAT scan to worry about. I was going to call you later this morning. I had a friend up in Manchester take a look at your pictures, and he couldn't find anything wrong. Says you're perfectly normal." The doctor forced a tired smile. " 'Course, he doesn't know you as well as I do, does he?"

Before Oliver could reply to the weak joke, an alarm sounded from beyond the double doors and Margolis hurried out. Oliver sank back onto the sagging Naugahyde sofa, then restlessly stood up and walked outside. Now, as he turned to go back into the waiting room, he saw Rebecca Morrison emerging through the double doors. Her eyes were red, and tears stained her cheeks. Hurrying back into the waiting room, he put his arms around her and held her close. "It's over?" he asked quietly, though he already knew the answer. He felt her nod, then she pulled back a little and looked up into his face.

"It was so strange," she said. "First she was breathing,

and I thought she was going to be all right, and then she wasn't. She just stopped breathing, Oliver. Why do things like that happen?"

"I don't know," Oliver said quietly. "It was just a terrible accident." He gently smoothed a lock of hair back from Rebecca's forehead, then brushed a tear from her cheek. "Sometimes things happen—" he began. Martha Ward's voice interrupted him.

"Things do not just happen," she declared. "There is such a thing as divine retribution, and it has been visited upon Andrea. God's will has been done. Rebecca, it is time for us to go home."

Oliver felt Rebecca freeze in his arms, then pull away from him.

"Yes, Aunt Martha," she said softly. "I'm sure Oliver will take us."

Nodding curtly to Oliver, Martha said, "You may take us home," then turned and without looking back strode out into the morning sun.

Rebecca was about to follow her, but Oliver held her back.

"What's going on?" he asked. "Does she even realize what's happened?"

Rebecca nodded. "She thinks Andrea was punished for getting an abortion. But I don't think God would do something like that, do you?"

Oliver shook his head. "And I don't think you ought to be living with her anymore, either. Isn't there some other place you can go? You could come and stay with me. I'll—"

"It's all right, Oliver," Rebecca said. "I can't leave Aunt Martha now. She doesn't have anyone else, and she's been so good to me for so long."

"But—"

"Please, Oliver? Just take us home?"

Five minutes later Oliver pulled into the driveway of Martha Ward's house. Amazingly, the only outward signs of the fire from this side of the house were the damage to the lawn and shrubbery, which had been inflicted by the hoses the firemen dragged from the trucks into the house and up to the second floor.

"You're sure you want to do this?" Oliver asked once again. "Even if the house is livable, it's going to smell—"

But Martha Ward was already out of the car and striding toward her house. As she reached the steps to the porch she turned back. "Come, Rebecca," she commanded.

Like a dog, Oliver thought angrily. She treats her like a dog.

But before he could say anything, Rebecca too had slipped out of the car, and a moment later both Martha and Rebecca disappeared inside.

Oliver knew he'd made a mistake as soon as he opened the door of the Red Hen. But he'd been so intent on satisfying the hunger in his stomach that he'd momentarily forgotten the equally strong hunger of the regular morning crowd who came to the diner to begin their day—not a hunger for the crullers and coffee for which the diner was famous, but a hunger for information.

"Information" was what they called it, since they were men. Their wives—far more accurately—would have called it "gossip."

Either way, almost every voice in the Red Hen fell silent as Oliver entered, and nearly every eye shifted to fix expectantly on him. After scanning the faces, he chose the table where Ed Becker and Bill McGuire were involved in a conversation that was suspended only long enough to beckon him over. As Oliver slid into the booth next to the attorney, Bill McGuire looked at him questioningly.

"Andrea Ward died about half an hour ago," he told them in answer to Bill's unspoken question.

The contractor winced. "What the hell's going on around here?" he asked.

Ed Becker signaled to the waitress for more coffee. "Nothing's going on," he said, and his tone was enough to tell Oliver that last night's fire wasn't all they'd been talking about.

McGuire shook his head dolefully as the waitress refilled his cup. "How can you say that?"

"Because it's true," the lawyer replied, then turned to Oliver. "Bill's starting to sound like he thinks there's some kind of curse on the town or something."

"I didn't say that," McGuire interjected a little too quickly.

"All right, maybe you didn't say it in those exact words," Becker conceded. "But when you start trying to connect a bunch of things that can't be connected, isn't some kind of curse what you're talking about?"

McGuire shook his head doggedly. "All I'm saying is that it's getting really weird around here. First the bank gets in trouble and Jules goes nuts and kills himself, and now Andrea Ward comes home after years away and burns to death the next day."

Though no one mentioned what had happened to Elizabeth McGuire, they didn't need to. Her suicide, so shortly preceding Jules Hartwick's, still hung over Bill like a specter, and though he hadn't spoken her name, he didn't have to.

"The fire was an accident, pure and simple," Oliver told the other two men. But after he'd filled them in on everything he'd learned over the past few hours, Bill McGuire was still shaking his head doubtfully.

"A few months ago I might have believed it wasn't anything more than Andrea falling asleep with a cigarette, but now . . ." His voice trailed off into a long sigh.

"Maybe it wasn't an accident," Ed Becker suggested. "Maybe Martha torched her."

"*Torched* her?" Oliver echoed, recoiling from the word. "Jesus, Ed, maybe you did criminal law too long. Why on earth would Martha Ward want to kill her own daughter?"

"Well, you said yourself she didn't seem to be too sorry Andrea had died. Didn't you say something about it being God's will?"

" 'Divine retribution,' was the way she put it," Oliver corrected him. "Martha's a religious fanatic. You know she sees the hand of God in practically everything."

"Sometimes people like that decide they *are* the hand of God," Becker said pointedly.

"Come on, Ed," Oliver said, lowering his voice and glancing around at the other patrons in the diner. "You know how gossip spreads around here. If anybody hears you, it'll be all over town by this afternoon."

"Let it!" Ed Becker said, leaning back and smiling mischievously. "Personally, I never could stand Martha Ward. Even when I was a kid, I always thought she wasn't just holier-than-thou. She was just plain mean. What I can't figure out is why Andrea came back at all."

"No place else to go, according to Rebecca," Oliver replied. He was about to tell them about the abortion Andrea had had yesterday, but stopped himself as he remembered that it was the miscarriage Bill's wife, Elizabeth, had suffered that led to her suicide, just days after losing their baby son. "I, on the other hand, *do* have places to go," he announced, sliding out of the booth. "And so does Bill, unless he's planning to drag the remodeling of my office out until all the problems at the bank are cleared up."

McGuire smiled for the first time that morning. "Finally figured it out, huh? Well, just don't tell your uncle, okay?"

Oliver eyed the contractor sardonically. "You think he

hasn't figured it out too? Why do you think he keeps coming up with new ideas every couple of weeks? Come on. Let's go figure out a whole new idea about what my office is going to look like, just on the off chance that Melissa Holloway gets the bank straightened out and you can finally get to work on the Center. And let's not talk about curses or dire plots, all right? I'm a journalist, not a fiction writer."

The two men hadn't been gone more than a minute before the Red Hen was once again buzzing with low voices, each of them passing on whatever scrap of Oliver's conversation they'd overheard.

Finally, Leonard Wilkins spoke. A crusty seventy, he had run the drive-in theater for thirty years before it closed and the grounds were given over to the flea market.

"You ask me," he said, "I think we should be keeping an eye on Oliver Metcalf."

"Come on," someone else said. "Oliver's solid as a rock."

"Maybe so," Wilkins replied. "But we still don't know just what it was that happened to his sister back when they were kids. Lately, since the trouble around here started, it seems to me that boy's been acting strange. And I heard from my Trudy that he was talking to Phil Margolis about headaches the other day. Bad headaches."

After only the shortest of pauses, the buzz in the diner resumed.

But now they were no longer talking about the fire that had killed Andrea Ward.

Now they were talking about Oliver Metcalf.

※

Chapter 9

*I*t wasn't just the look of the room, though that was bad enough. The bed—the one Rebecca had slept in nearly every night of the last twelve years—was a sodden, blackened ruin. Even from the doorway—Rebecca hadn't yet found the courage to actually go into the room—she could see that the fire must have started in the bed and spread from there. She shuddered as she imagined Andrea falling asleep, a cigarette between her fingers. The cigarette must have dropped onto the coverlet, slowly burned its way through the blankets, sheets, and pad, and eventually burrowed into the mattress itself.

But why hadn't Andrea awakened? Wouldn't she have begun choking on the smoke filling the room? Or had she just gone from sleep directly into unconsciousness, utterly oblivious to what was happening to her? She must have, or surely she would have awakened as the fire had spread out from the bed, crawling across the carpet, then climbing up the curtains around the windows. The paint on the window frames was badly charred, and the wallpaper hung in scorched shreds. Everything in the room would have to go, and the paper and paint peeled down to the bare wood.

It was the smell that truly made Rebecca shiver. The terrible smell that was nothing like the friendly odor of a fire burning on a hearth. This was an odor she would never forget. From the moment she and her aunt had come back into the house, it filled her nostrils, every breath bringing back the memory of awakening in the middle of the night and realizing that the house was on fire.

Though Martha Ward objected, Rebecca had gone through every room of the house save the chapel, opening the windows as wide as she could and propping open all the doors to prevent any of them from blowing shut and cutting off the breeze. The cold air was eliminating at least the worst of the acrid smell. She'd stripped her bed, and her aunt's too, and put the linens into the big washing machine down in the basement, but even as she began the first batch of laundry, she'd known that it was going to be endless. Every piece of clothing would have to be washed, every stick of furniture cleaned. Every rug would have to be taken to the cleaners. Even then, she was certain the smell would remain, which meant that every time she entered the house, the whole terrifying scene from last night would come back to her like a nightmare from which she would never escape.

She was still standing at the door to Andrea's room, willing herself to go in, when she heard her aunt calling to her from downstairs: "Rebecca? Rebecca! This house won't get clean by itself."

Rebecca was about to turn away from the door to Andrea's room when something caught her eye.

Something that glittered in odd contrast to the charred blackness of the room.

Something that was almost hidden beneath the bed.

Even as she went into the room to pick the object up, she knew what it was.

The cigarette lighter she'd given Andrea the day before yesterday, in the shape of a dragon's head.

Wiping away the worst of the soot, she turned the shining object over in her hands. The dragon's red eyes glared up at her, and though there were still some smudges of soot on the creature's golden scales, it seemed undamaged by the fire.

When she pressed the trigger in its neck, a tongue of flame immediately appeared.

"Rebecca? Rebecca! I am waiting for you!"

Her aunt's commanding voice startled her, and Rebecca scurried out of the ruined room and down the stairs. Martha was waiting in the foyer, a bucket of soapy water at her feet. She handed Rebecca a rag. "Start here. I shall start in the kitchen."

Rebecca glanced at the soot-stained paper on the walls. "It will ruin the paper, Aunt Martha."

"The paper will not be ruined," Martha pronounced. "The Lord will cleanse our house as surely as He punished Andrea for her sins." Then her eyes fell on the object in Rebecca's hand. "What is that?" she demanded.

Rebecca's first impulse was to slip the dragon into her pocket, to keep it out of her aunt's sight, but she knew it was already too late. Reluctantly, she placed the golden dragon in her aunt's hand. "It's just a cigarette lighter," she said softly. "I gave it to Andrea on Sunday, when she came back."

Martha Ward held the lighter up, turning it and examining it from every angle. "Where did this come from?" she asked, her eyes still fixed on the dragon.

"The flea market," Rebecca replied. "Oliver and I found it, and—"

"Oliver?" Martha cut in. "Oliver Metcalf?"

Rebecca shrank back from the opprobrium in her aunt's voice. "Oliver is my friend," she said, but the words were uttered so quietly they were almost inaudible.

"I might have expected Oliver Metcalf to find something like this," Martha said, her fingers tightening around the dragon for a moment before she deposited it in the pocket of her apron. "I shall dispose of this."

"But it's not yours, Aunt Martha. I gave it to Andrea, and—" Her voice broke. "And I'd just—well, I'd just like to keep it."

Martha Ward's expression hardened into the same

dark mask of condemnation that had appeared on her face at dinner the evening before, when Andrea told her what she'd done in Boston. "It is a graven image, and a tool of the Devil," she pronounced. "I shall decide how best to dispose of it."

She turned away and disappeared down the hall toward the kitchen.

Rebecca dipped the rag into the bucket of soapy water, wrung it out, and began wiping the layer of soot from the woodwork around the front door. But even as she worked she knew it was useless. No matter how long they might scrub, the terrible stench of the fire would never be removed from the house.

But her aunt, she also knew, would never let her stop trying.

Chapter 10

*I*n the silence of the night, Martha Ward moved slowly through the rooms of her house. She had lived in it all her life; the past was hidden in every corner. It had been years since she'd gone in search of the memories though, having long since confined herself to the rooms in which she felt safest.

Her room. Not her parents' room, where she and Fred Ward had slept in the few short years before he deserted her, but her own childhood room, where she'd lived when she was still an innocent, before she allowed herself to be tempted into sin. The room she'd moved back into the day Fred Ward left, to tempt her no more.

She had been lucky, or so she'd thought. She, at least, had married Fred Ward before allowing him to lead her away from the path of righteousness.

Not like her younger sister, who had given birth to Rebecca only five months after marrying Mick Morrison.

And certainly not like her older sister, who had allowed Tommy Gardner to show her the ways of evil, and never married her at all.

In the course of her bitter catechism, Martha had come to understand the wages of sin, and all the forms of retribution that God's will could take.

Certainly His divine will had been visited on her family many times over the years, and in many ways.

First, there was her older sister, who had been banished from the house as soon as her sin was discovered. But

Martha herself was a small child then, and hadn't understood Marilyn's sin. She had simply thought her sister was sick, and that was why she'd been taken to the hospital on the top of the hill. Finally, after Marilyn had been gone a very long time, Martha opened her piggy bank, took out all the money, and bought her sister a present. It was a cigarette lighter, and to her six-year-old eyes it had been beautiful, with its golden scales and its ruby eyes. She had gazed lovingly at it before taking it up to the front door of the big stone hospital and giving it to the first person she'd seen, who had promised to deliver it to her sister.

Her father had been very angry when he found out what she'd done. He'd beaten her, and kept her in her room for a week, and when finally she'd been allowed out, he told her that she would never see her sister again.

It wasn't until years later that she finally learned what had happened to her sister, and when she'd gone to her priest to confess the sin of having given her sister the instrument with which Marilyn had killed herself, the priest had reassured her. "It was God's will," he told her. "Your sister sinned grievously, and the gift you offered her was no more than a tool of divine intervention. You are blessed, for God chose to act through you."

Though her older sister had been promptly punished for her sin, Martha's younger sister's punishment had not been meted out by the hand of God for sixteen years. Yet when the "accident" had finally come, Martha quickly understood that it had been no accident at all. In the flickering candlelight of the chapel, with the Gregorian chants numbing her mind to all other sound but God's voice, Martha had quickly come to understand that Rebecca's parents had finally been punished for their sin. She had also understood that it was her duty to take Rebecca—the fruit of that long-ago sin—into her home and shelter her from the ways of evil.

Martha had done her best to do just that.

She had given Rebecca her own daughter's room, and tried to keep her on the path from which even Andrea had strayed.

Two of the rooms—the room in which her parents, and even she and Fred Ward, had lain together, and the room in which Rebecca's mother had lain with Mick Morrison—she refused to set foot in. Others, such as the dining room and living room, which her parents had used for entertaining their godless friends, she simply avoided.

Rebecca kept them clean of course, for Martha had been careful in her instruction of the girl, instilling in her not only the virtue of chastity but of cleanliness as well.

For herself, Martha used only her childhood bedroom, where she knew no sin had ever been committed, and the chapel, in which she prayed for salvation and the guidance to keep herself and Rebecca free of sin.

And it had been working. As the years of prayer and devotion went by, Martha slowly felt a purity coming into the house, the same purity she felt in her own blessed soul, and she had grown secure in the knowledge that she, at least, was safe from the damnation that had befallen both her sisters.

Two days ago, when Andrea—unbidden and unwelcome—had returned, Martha knew she should have closed her doors to her, refused even to look upon her harlot's face. But she had not. Instead she allowed Andrea to enter the house, and Satan had slipped in with her.

Adultery with a married man.

A child unblessed by wedlock.

Abortion!

Why had she tolerated it?

And now, as she roamed sleeplessly through the rooms of the house, all the memories came back. In the living room she could still feel her older sister's presence, even smell the perfume she'd used to draw the Devil—in the form of Tommy Gardner—near.

In the big bedroom upstairs, unused for decades, she could hear her younger sister's moans of pleasure as she'd given herself to the false joys of sin in the arms of Mick Morrison.

Despite Martha's years of prayer and atonement, Satan still resided here. Even the smell of the smoke from the fire in which Andrea had died couldn't cover the stench of sin, which drenched the house in a sulfurous fog.

Finally, Martha went into the chapel. Lighting all the candles, she turned on the music of the Gregorian chants, keeping it soft enough not to awaken Rebecca, then sank onto the prie-dieu. The rosary draped from her fingers, she began silently reciting the decades of her prayers. As the candles flickered and the chanting droned, she opened her mind to the voice of God and fixed her eyes on the face of her Savior. But as the minutes of prayer ticked by and slowly turned into hours, the face that Martha Ward beheld began to change.

The face of her Savior was transfigured, and now she was gazing into the eyes of the dragon.

As she gazed deep into the ruby eyes, a voice came to her, and told her what she must do.

Martha Ward rose and left the chapel.

Rebecca ignored the first drop of water that fell onto her face. It was a perfect spring day, the kind she loved the best, when the sun was shining brightly in a soft blue sky, the trees were covered with the pale green of newly spreading leaves, the last of the crocuses were still in bloom, and the barely opened daffodils were showing the first traces of yellow. Birds were singing and a gentle breeze was blowing, carrying the pungent fragrance of the pine woods behind the house through her window, and she breathed deeply of it. Sighing, she shifted her position, squirming contentedly under her light coverlet.

Another drop hit her face, and then another.

Rain?

But how could it be rain?

She was in her room, and even though the window was open and a cool breeze was wafting in, she could see that the morning sky was perfectly clear.

But then another drop hit her face, and yet another.

She squirmed again, then rolled over, trying to escape the rain that was spoiling the perfect morning.

The sunlight was fading away, and as darkness gathered around her, the breeze died, and with it the pine scent it had carried. The fresh, perfumed air she had thrilled to only a moment ago now had an acrid quality to it that made her want to turn her head away.

Even the rain had changed; it no longer felt like rain at all.

The birdsong had shifted too, dropping from the merry tune of a moment ago into a low murmur of sounds that were familiar but not quite identifiable.

She rolled over again. Suddenly she was coughing and choking. Her nostrils were flooded with the acrid odor. She jerked awake and the last remnants of the dream gave way to consciousness.

It wasn't morning at all: the only light in the room came from the moon that hung low in the sky outside.

Nor had she felt a breeze, for the window was tightly closed against the cold March night.

But the rain? What had caused her to dream of rain?

Then she realized that the bedding around her was cold and wet, clammy with something that smelled like . . .

Turpentine?

But it wasn't possible. Why would—

Only then did she notice the movement in the room, and hear the muttering that in her dream had sounded like the singing of birds.

Her heart pounding, Rebecca freed herself of the clinging bedding and groped for the switch on the small reading lamp on the table next to the daybed. She blinked in the glare, but then her eyes focused and she recognized her aunt.

Her eyes wide and unblinking, gazing into the distance upon something that Rebecca couldn't see at all, Martha Ward was moving around the room, pouring turpentine from a large can onto the curtains and the walls. The smell of it was so strong that it utterly obliterated the smoky odor that had filled the room when Rebecca went to sleep. Instinctively, Rebecca clutched the sheet to her nose and mouth to filter out the noxious fumes, only to begin coughing once again. As her gorge rose in response to the bitter taste of the turpentine she'd sucked into her mouth, she shoved the soaked covers away.

"Aunt Martha, don't!" she begged, the words rasping in her throat. "What are—"

She left the question unfinished as she realized her aunt was as deaf to her voice as she seemed blind to the light that Rebecca had turned on.

"Cleansed," she heard her aunt muttering. "We must be cleansed of our sins that we may live in the presence of the Lord!"

Shaking the last of the turpentine from the can, Martha hesitated for a moment, looking at the container almost as if she didn't understand why the fluid had stopped flowing from it. Then she turned abruptly and strode from the room, pulling the pocket doors to the dining room closed behind her.

A second later Rebecca heard the click of the lock as her aunt twisted the key.

Leaping from the bed, Rebecca ran to the doors, pulled and pounded, trying to pry them open.

"Aunt Martha!" Fear bloomed in her as she realized she was trapped in the little room. "Aunt Martha, let me out!"

Instead of a response to her pleas, Rebecca heard only the sound of her aunt's mumbled prayers, now muffled by the thick wood of the closed and locked doors.

Out!

She had to get out, and get help!

Snatching her bathrobe from the hook in the little room's single tiny closet, Rebecca pulled it on, jammed her feet into a pair of worn sneakers, then ran to the window. Though the lock at the top of the lower casement finally turned, the window frame had long ago been painted shut. No matter how hard she tried, Rebecca couldn't jerk it loose. Finally she picked up the small reading lamp, smashed the lower pane, then knocked the broken shards away until it was safe for her to climb out. Dropping to the ground only a few feet below, she hesitated.

Where was she going to go?

Memories flashed through her mind—memories of the strange looks her aunt's neighbors, the VanDeventers, had given her over the years; of remarks they'd made when they thought she couldn't hear them.

Poor Rebecca.

Hasn't been quite right since the accident.

Afraid it left her just a little bit touched in the head.

What would they say if she pounded on their doors in the middle of the night, saying her aunt was going to burn her house down?

Oliver!

Oliver would listen to her! He was her friend, and he didn't think she was crazy!

Instead of heading for the front of the house, Rebecca ran across the backyard to the edge of the woods, where a narrow trail edged the Hartwicks', then hooked up with the path that led to the Asylum. Though there were still a few clouds in the sky, there was enough moonlight so Rebecca was able to run all but the few yards where the path was so soggy and muddy that she had to slow almost to a stop and pick her way through. By the time she arrived at Oliver's front door and began pounding and shouting to him, her sneakers were sodden and heavy with mud, and her legs were streaked with it as well. The cold night air had long since penetrated the thin material of her bathrobe, and though she was panting from running, she was shivering from the cold as well.

When there was no immediate response to her pounding on the door, Rebecca pressed her finger on the bell, banged once more, then stepped back to shout up toward the second floor. "Oliver! Oliver, wake up! It's Rebecca!"

It seemed like forever before the porch light came on, the front door was thrown open, and Oliver peered out. "Rebecca? What is it? What—"

Rebecca, finally overcome by the cold, the darkness, and the terror she'd only barely been able to control long enough to get there, began sobbing. "She locked me in," she began. "She tried ... I mean she wants ..." She paused, forced herself to take a deep breath, then lost control again.

Oliver pulled her into the house and closed the door, shutting out the cold. "It's all right, Rebecca," he soothed. "You're safe now. Just try to tell me what happened."

"It's Aunt Martha," Rebecca finally managed to say. "She's ... oh, Oliver, I think she's gone crazy!"

Chapter 11

*A*ll was ready.

Save for her beloved Gregorian chants, the only music that had ever been able to soothe her soul, Martha Ward's house was silent.

Though she harbored a vague memory of Rebecca calling out to her a while ago, her niece's voice had quickly fallen silent.

God's hand, Martha was certain, had muted the sinful girl.

She gazed at herself in the mirror one last time— chiding herself for her vanity, but secure in the knowledge that she would be forgiven, as she would be forgiven all her sins in a few more minutes—and smiled, recognizing how beautiful she looked.

The image in the mirror perfectly reflected Martha's vision of herself: her youth restored, her cheeks rosy and her lips full, her eyes wide and filled with childlike innocence. Though her dress had been worn once before—the day she'd married Fred Ward—in the mirror it appeared as pristinely new as the day she'd bought it, and indeed, as she gazed at the seed pearls scattered across its bosom, and the perfect virtue expressed in its flowing expanse of pure white, its long sleeves and high neck, she had no memory of ever having seen it before.

A tiara of pearls held a veil to her head, and as she pulled the thin layer of tulle down over her face, Martha's image took on an ethereal, almost saintly quality. Satisfied that all was in order, she turned at last away from the mirror and from vanity itself, knowing she would never look at her reflection again. Picking up the single object she would carry to the ceremony awaiting her, she left her bedroom, gently closing the door behind her.

Downstairs she paused outside the chapel, composed herself, then opened the door and let herself inside. The room was dark but for a single perfect light shining on the face of Christ, which seemed to float in the darkness above the altar. Genuflecting deeply, Martha moved slowly toward the altar, her eyes never leaving the face that hovered above her. Finally, when she was very close to the altar, she squeezed the object in her hands with trembling fingers.

A tongue of fire leaped from the dragon's mouth.

Holding tight to the gilded beast, she began to light the candles on the altar, moving steadily from one to another, uttering a silent prayer over each.

She prayed for her mother and her father.

For her elder sister, Marilyn, whose sins had taken her to an early death.

For Tommy Gardner, whom Satan had sent to tempt Marilyn.

For Margaret and Mick Morrison, the fruit of whose sin Martha herself had taken into her home.

The dragon's tongue touched candle after candle, for Martha knew well that Blackstone was filled with sinners, and on this night above all others, redemption must be begged for each of them.

When all the candles on the altar were glowing brightly, Martha turned to the saints in their alcoves, lighting a candle for each of them, that they might bear witness to the glory of this night.

Martha lit the candles in front of the Blessed Virgin, kneeling in front of the statue and praying that she might be found worthy of the saint's only son.

When all the prayers were said, Martha rose to her feet once more. She started once again toward the altar, hesitated, then realized there was one more thing she must do.

Going first to one of the windows, then the other, she drew back the heavy draperies, securing them carefully with the velvet ties that had hung unused for more than two decades. She opened the sheers as well, and though the rotted material tore to shreds in her fingers, she was unaware of anything but the glory of her surroundings, open at last to the world outside so that anyone who wished might watch and bear witness to her final salvation. As she returned to face the altar and her Savior this ultimate time, she was utterly unaware of the siren that had started to wail outside and the lights that were going on in her neighbors' homes as they rose from their beds to see what new tragedy might have befallen their town.

Dropping to her knees, Martha silently began the vows that would tie her to her Savior for all eternity.

Oliver Metcalf's Volvo pulled up to the curb in front of Martha Ward's house only seconds after the police car whose siren had already awakened the neighbors. As Rebecca tried to explain her aunt's strange behavior to Steve Driver, the occupants of the neighboring houses began to appear, some of them still clad in their night-clothes, others having pulled on overcoats, still others having hastily dressed. They clustered around Rebecca, whispering to each other as first one, then another, picked up a fragment of the peculiar tale she was relating. But even before she had finished, someone noticed the two windows that were glowing brightly in the otherwise darkened house.

Swept along with the gathering of neighbors, Rebecca and Oliver moved closer to the Hartwicks' driveway, their gazes following those of everyone else. Through the uncurtained windows they could clearly see Martha

Ward standing in her wedding dress in front of her altar, her veiled face tilted upward, her entire figure bathed in the golden glow of the flickering candles.

"What's she doing?" someone asked.

No one answered.

Her vows completed, Martha Ward knelt one last time. Her eyes still fixed on the face of the figure above the altar, her fingers tightened on the dragon's neck.

For the last time the dragon's flame came alive.

Martha Ward reached down and touched the reptile's tongue to the turpentine-soaked carpet. As the flames spread quickly around her, she cast the dragon from her hand and rose once more to her full height. Lifting the veil from her face, she felt herself filled with a rapturous exaltation. As the fire consumed her sins, she felt her spirit being uplifted, and she raised her arms in unutterable joy.

As the medieval voices of her beloved chants gave way to the crackling of the spreading flames, Martha Ward's soul rose to meet the destiny for which she had always prayed.

"Don't watch it," Oliver said. He drew Rebecca to him, pressing her face into his shoulder to shield her from the horror unfolding within the house.

A silence descended upon the crowd as they watched Martha Ward's last moments, a silence now broken by a gasp as flames suddenly rose around her. As the fire grew, some of the women began to sob and some of the men swore softly, but no one made any move to stop the fire, to put an end to the conflagration that was already spreading through the house, destroying everything in its path.

More sirens tore apart the night, but even when the volunteer engines arrived, their crews did nothing to quench the flames, but only stood by to protect the homes next door.

Within minutes the entire structure was engulfed, the heat enough to drive even the bravest to the opposite side of the street. Finally the entire structure collapsed in upon itself, and a tower of sparks rose into the night sky as if in some strange and macabre celebration.

A pile of smoldering rubble was all that remained of Martha Ward's house.

As dawn broke, Oliver watched in fascination while the crowd that had gathered in the night to watch the fire quickly dispersed, as if they felt exposed by the morning light and were embarrassed to have the morbidness of their curiosity further revealed.

The firemen were circling the wreckage of the house like a band of hunters warily inspecting fallen prey, knowing it was mortally wounded, but all too aware that it was still capable of inflicting damage upon anyone who ventured too close.

"Do you have any place to go?" Oliver finally asked Rebecca. She was next to him, her hand holding on to his arm, but her eyes still fixed on the blackened ruin that had been her home. For a long time she said nothing, and he was about to repeat the question when he heard a voice behind him.

"She'll come to live with me. It's what her aunt would have wanted."

Turning, Oliver saw Germaine Wagner standing a few feet away, a gray woolen overcoat buttoned up to her neck, a grayer scarf wrapped around her head.

Oliver turned back to Rebecca, whose wide, frightened eyes made it clear she had no idea what to do. "You can stay with me if you'd like," he said softly. "'' have an extra room."

Rebecca glanced uncertainly at Germaine Wagner, then back to Oliver, but before she could say anything, the librarian spoke again.

"That's not a good idea, Oliver. You know as well as I do that it would cause talk." Her lips pursed disapprovingly. "The very idea—you and Rebecca? It's—" She hesitated, and Oliver wondered if she was going to finish her thought. But then her eyes fixed on his. "Well, you know what I mean, don't you? Surely I don't have to spell it out for you."

Just as they had in the library on the December day when he'd gone in to research the Asylum's history under Germaine's stern stare, the old memories now rushed back at him once again, memories of the people who used to glance at him out of the corner of their eye and whisper about him behind his back. If Rebecca came to live with him, would it all start up again?

Of course it would.

The only difference would be that this time the whispers would be about Rebecca instead of his sister.

For himself, it didn't really matter. But for Rebecca?

He wouldn't put her through it.

"No," he said at last, "you don't have to spell it out for me."

He watched in silence as Germaine Wagner led Rebecca toward her car, and wondered if she was also walking away from him forever. Sighing heavily, he realized that if Germaine had anything to do with it, she might very well be.

A few minutes later, as he too drove away from the wreckage of Martha Ward's house, Oliver realized that his head was starting to ache again.

This time, though, he was fairly sure he knew the reason why.

Enough rain had fallen on Blackstone in the weeks since Martha Ward had turned the tongue of the dragon upon herself that the smell of the fire had finally begun to be washed away, its acrid stench slowly replaced with the sweet aroma of the first flowers of spring. Behind the thick stone walls of the Asylum, though, the same stale, musty odor of mildew and mold that had permeated every hidden corner of the building for the last several decades still hung heavily in the air.

The dankness was of no concern to the dark figure that moved through the shadowed rooms, as oblivious to the still and moldering atmosphere within the walls as he was to the freshly vibrant breezes beyond.

He was in his museum once more, carefully—almost lovingly—pasting Oliver Metcalf's account of Martha Ward's last moments into the leather-bound ledger he had found two months ago. Satisfied with his work only when his latex-covered fingers had perfectly trimmed every edge and smoothed out every wrinkle, he read the story one more time, then put the cherished book aside.

Now, before the full moon began to fade, it was time to decide which of his treasures next to give away. His fingers moved over them slowly and sensuously, feeling the details his eyes could not discern in the dim light, until at last he came to the one he knew should next be sent to work its evil.

A handkerchief, woven from the finest linen, edged in the daintiest of lace, and perfectly embroidered with a single ornate initial.

An initial that would guide this cherished article to its target as surely as if it were an arrow shot from a bow.

To be continued . . .

The serial thriller continues next month . . .

JOHN SAUL'S
THE BLACKSTONE CHRONICLES:
Part Four
In the Shadow of Evil: The Handkerchief

Ever since plans to demolish the old Asylum were delayed, various members of the small town of Blackstone have received mysterious gifts from an unknown hand. Each item carries a hideous hidden power to harm. Who is responsible for these dark harbingers of death? And who will have the misfortune to find a delicately embroidered handkerchief? The cantankerous Clara Wagner . . . her haughty daughter, Germaine, the town librarian . . . the editor of the local paper, Oliver Metcalf . . . or the soft-spoken object of his affection, Rebecca Morrison?

One person will recall a jarring, horrific memory, another will die a gruesome death. . . .

To be continued . . .

THE PRESENCE
by John Saul

With every one of his spine-tingling novels of
psychological and supernatural suspense, *New
York Times* bestselling author John Saul has
given readers a variety of chilling reasons to
sleep with the lights on. Now brace yourself for
his most terrifying novel yet. Have you ever felt
that frightening feeling that someone—or something—is following you, only to discover when
you turn around that there's nothing there? Be
warned: You are not alone. . . .

BEWARE
THE PRESENCE!

Coming this summer
A Fawcett Columbine
Hardcover Book